PLAY BY PLAY

Also by Isaac Goldemberg

The Fragmented Life
of Don Jacobo Lerner (NOVEL)

Hombre de Paso/
Just Passing Through (POEMS)

Isaac Goldemberg

PLAY BY PLAY

Translated from the Spanish
by Hardie St. Martin

Persea Books • New York

To Dina and David: always.

For information, address the publisher:

Persea Books
225 Lafayette Street
New York, N.Y. 10012

The publication of this book has been supported in part by grants from the National Endowment for the Arts and the New York State Council on the Arts.

Designed by Peter St. John Ginna
Set in Bookman and Italia by Keystrokes, Lenox, Massachusetts

Printed in the United States of America by The Book Press, Brattleboro, Vermont.

FIRST HALF

FIVETHOUSANDSEVENHUNDRED and thirteen years of Judaism hit Marquitos Karushansky like a ton of bricks. At the age of eight, shortly after coming to Lima, classes in Hebrew and the history of the Jews at León Pinelo School; bris at the age of twelve; Bar Mitzvah at thirteen when he was a brand-new cadet at Leoncio Prado Military Academy. Bris was the little word taken from the Hebrew and used by the Jews in Lima to avoid saying circumcision, which left a bad taste in the mouth and made them bite the tip of their tongues, as if to spit it out. "Never you say circumcision, correct word is bris; circumcision is from Latin circumcidere, to cut around, and has no historical weight. But bris means covenant and is in Bible from time our father Abruhem sealed pact with Adonai."

That's how Rabbi Goldstein, with his weeping willow beard, explained it to him. Adonai, of course, was also a word Marcos had recently picked up. Saying God, which seemed to have a cholo, half-Indian ring to it, was absolutely out of the question. And it was really something to watch him swearing, Chai Adonai here and Chai Adonai there! whip 'em in the front and whip 'em in the rear! Chahuee! Chahuaa! Pinelo, Pinelo, rah, rah, rah! First you've got to promise not to tell. I swear to God who is my shining light! What? To God! No, that doesn't count. C'mon, do it right. Chai Adonai! You're a liar, let's see if you can swear it's true. Chai Adonai! Swear you didn't steal the ballpoint. Chai Adonai! Marcos gradually became used to the word, it was like not swearing at all, and he got a big kick out of it.

Marquitos Karushansky's circumcision, or rather his bris, took place on the same day as the opening of The Ten Commandments at the Tacna movie theater. What's more, Dr. Berkowitz's office, where the operation was done, was only half a block from the theater. Marcos was operated on in the afternoon, some time between five and seven, and the show was to start at eight. But he and his father missed the opening. The saddest part of it, old Karushansky said, was not being able to see the film together with the rest of the Jewish community of Lima. They had to see it four or five days later, sitting among Peruvians, and it wasn't the same, it wasn't the right atmosphere, what did those cholos know about the Bible, anyway?

It had all started when his father announced,

like a patriarch in the Old Testament: "Next year you be ready for Bar Mitzvah but first is necessary you have bris." Marcos remembered his eyes wandering to the smudgy windowpane, and then his voice, mocking and at the same time trying to reassure him, he shouldn't worry, they had also snipped off the foreskin of Jesus the Jew.

They showed up one day in Dr. Berkowitz's office where the physician, very professional, very freckled, explained: "Bris is an extremely simple operation. All it amounts to is cutting off the prepuce, the end of the skin that folds over the head of the penis and covers it. Then it's much easier to keep the glans clean. No sebaceous matter collects around it and this reduces the risk of catching dangerous infections." Marcos didn't know what he was talking about and went back with his father to the doctor's office the next day. The nurse had already left and they were greeted by a silence like the Sabbath's in the homes of Orthodox Jews. Before he knew it, Marcos was stretched out on his back on the operating table. Dr. Berkowitz was standing beside it, scalpel in hand, arm poised, and his father, sweat running down features drawn tight in pain and disgust, his father was lying across his chest, pinning his arms, papa's chunky body on top of his, would he ask him for a camphor liniment rubdown later? Every night at bedtime the ritual of the rubdown would begin and Marcos would massage him furiously, as if he wanted to tear off his skin, as if he were trying to draw blood from the heavy body with an oval head. He would pass the palm of his hand down the slope of the thick short neck, up the incline of the shoulders with their overgrowth of hair, matted like the fur on a battered old grizzly, his body stripped of every shred of nobility, letting out low grunts, soft moans of pleasure.

His penis had been put to sleep but not enough to kill the pain from the clamp holding on to his skin as if it would never let go. Then the doctor—warning him not to exaggerate, because too much anesthetic could leave him paralyzed for life—raised the needle to eye level to make sure he had the right amount in the syringe. His whole body shuddered when the needle entered his glans. His father pressed all his weight down on his chest, and on his lips and chin Marcos could feel the rough beard, soaked with sweat and tears. Now his penis was a soft mass, a spongy mushroom, an organism with a life of its own, capable of tearing free with one jerk and slipping all over his skin, looking for a way into his body, or capable of dissolving and leaving a smelly, viscous fluid on his groin. He knew his penis was already in the open and he tried to imagine its new, hoodless look. In his mind, he compared it to the image he had of his father's member, its extreme whiteness, the perfect distribution of its parts, the scarlet crest topping the head of the sleepy iguana, with its vertical blind eye. He wanted to examine his phallus, to hold it above his eyes like a flower, to fall under the spell of the rosy calyx snug around its neck, to weigh it in his hand and stroke it warmly back to the familiarity it had lost. He was conscious of the small pincers clutching his foreskin tight: they were fierce little animals with fangs, beady eyes, and metallic scales on their backs. At the same time, he felt the pressure of his father's dead weight on him as a reproach, the embodiment of all the insults he had ever had to take. He thought about how, when he went back to school, he wouldn't have to hide from his friends in the bathroom. He would be able to piss casually now, to pull out his prick, take his time shaking it out, boldly pressing hard to squeeze the last drops out and then turn around defiantly and show it to the others, to all his schoolmates at León Pinelo, proudly, now let's see who is man enough to say I'm not a Jew.

The doctor left them alone in the back office: he told them he'd return in half an hour, they'd have to wait for the anesthetic to wear off, and Marcos watched his father nodding yes. Then the old man started to pace with his hands clasped behind him. He marched up and down next to the operating table, eyes straight ahead, without bending his knees, swinging each leg sideways slowly in a semicircle, before setting his foot down on the tiles. The controlled stiffness of his body, the deliberate halt after each about-face, before he started pacing again, reflected all the misery and resignation stored up in him. But Marcos knew every detail of this tactic his father had used, over the past two years, to put a certain amount of distance between them, to make him understand that behind this temporary withdrawal, all the things he had ever silenced were crying out, louder than words, against his bad luck and his unhappiness. If he had had any hope of crossing into his father's world, he would have asked him to come over to the table, dry the sweat on his forehead, take his hand in his, and help him clear away the skein of solitude unraveling endlessly in his chest. But he was sure the old man would avoid his eyes, as he did whenever he pounded on him with his fists, only to feel sorry afterward and break down like a vulnerable Mary Magdalene.

His senses had become dulled. His father looked older now: his beard had taken on a grayish tint and a hundred wrinkles had formed around his eyes. He tried to think of his mother but he couldn't retain a solid image of her behind his eyes. He had closed them and felt himself rushing down a toboggan run, rolling over and over without being able to stop. Only his father was solid; all the objects in the room had melted into ribbons of vapor swirling around him, and only his father's presence kept him from turning into a gaseous substance too.

He didn't move a muscle when the doctor's voice burst into the room like a garble of voices and sounds, and asked him if he was feeling better. He nodded without unlocking his eyelids, and the doctor and his father helped him off the table. His eyes were still closed, he staggered as if whipped by a blizzard, and the weight of his nakedness embarrassed him. The mere brush of the doctor's gloved hands on his member, the slight pull of the threads sticking out from the skin under the glans, made him feel wretched and he had the urge to piss. He guessed the pain this rash move would bring on and stopped himself just in time; the doc-

tor was fitting a jockstrap stuffed with wads of gauze on him and he had the sensation that he was pissing inward. His bladder was tightening up and his inward-flowing urine plunged through his ureters, was picked up by the renal tubes, flooded his kidneys like a winding current, and was pumped, bubbling and humming, into the bloodstream. He felt that he was burning up inside, explored by the fine probe of an intense blue flame. The doctor's voice jolted him back to reality. A sudden smile lit up the doctor's face as he put out his hand in an outlandishly formal way and made a big show of shaking Marcos's father's hand, saying: "Mazel tov, Señor Karushansky, congratulations, mazel tov . . ."

The lights on Tacna Avenue woke him all the way. Walking to the corner, they passed the Tacna movie theater, its front covered with giant posters showing scenes from the movie: a beardless Charlton Heston, dressed as an Egyptian warrior, was giving a wasp-waisted princess a he-man's hug; over to the right, Charlton Heston again, beard and wig, tunic and sandals, on a promontory, arms extended like a magician's: abracadabra, let the waters divide.

As they stood on the corner trying to get a cab, Marcos thought of the late afternoon when he had arrived in Lima, four years before. Through the smoke rising steadily from a charcoal pit where some shish kebab on tiny skewers was roasting and giving off a tempting aroma, he saw his father with his hands in his pockets, coming toward the El Chasqui travel agency, where he and his mother were waiting. Then, like now, they had stopped on a corner, loaded down with bundles and suitcases, to get a cab. He looked out the side of his eye at his father, sitting cross-legged next to him; his arms were folded stiffly across his chest. Through the window on the other side of his father's aquiline profile, he watched the streetcars stretching, lumbering over the flashing tracks. Tall buildings loomed up unexpectedly, swaying like the carob trees back home, and then, with the speed of a fist coming straight at his eyes out of nowhere, the slender pyramid of the Jorge Chávez monument like an airplane full of lights—manned by a crew of graceful winged granite figures—taking off into the night.

He had seen pictures of the Plaza San Martín and the Plaza de Armas in his schoolbook and had thought of Lima as a ghost town where time had stopped without warning, freezing cars as they moved along and pedestrians as they walked. He liked to invent all kinds of stories about those unknown people suspended in midair like grotesque puppets. He had even tried to see if he could make out his father among those men in dark suits and hats. Sometimes he felt sure he had found him sitting on a bench reading a newspaper, or spotted his profile coming around a corner, and he would run to the kitchen and point him out to his mother. Without hiding her amazement at her son's fancies, she would stroke his head nervously and always tell him no, with an understanding smile. But now, sitting on his father's right, he didn't have to imagine him anymore. The city itself seemed to have come out of its sleep, happy to open the night and show him his father's world. And with all his senses set on the course of this moment so new to him, fluttering around him like a playful butterfly, he accepted that world unquestioning, wholeheartedly, as if it had always been his by right.

The taxi plunged into the warm shadows of a Salaverry Avenue studded with lights. His father was still just sitting there, his face outlined by the pale flash of the car's window, oblivious of the clusters of trees reflected in his eyes as they shot past. On the right, the Campo de Marte spread out; deserted, bleak, it disappeared for stretches at a time behind groups of houses and reappeared, somnolent and hazy. Marcos was quiet too, afraid to shift a leg that had fallen asleep and trying with his imagination to lop it off from his body and stop the swirl of bubbles climbing to his groin slowly, noisily. He let the stale air out of his lungs and sank a little into the seat, thinking That old guy is my father, I can tell by the musty odor of his clothes, he smells like dirty synagogue draperies, old velvet, damp wool, like the moth-eaten cashmere and poplin remnants he keeps in back of the store. He's probably taking the annual inventory right now, setting bolts of cloth on the counter, running his hand over them like a shepherd fondly stroking the backs of his sheep; or maybe he's repeating over and over the words he spit out at me this morning, "In a few hours you be at last one of us, at last one of us, at last one . . ."

As the cab made a sharp turn, coming out into Mariátegui Avenue, its chassis seemed to bristle up like a cat; it went down the street chugging along unsteadily, entered Pumacahua Street and pulled up at the corner of the second block, where the houses came to a dead end, cut off by the Club Hípico's garden wall, a solid line of trees and wire. His father helped him out of the car. They walked the short distance to the project entrance and silently headed for the apartment at the rear.

In the bedroom his father helped him undress; he knelt to take off his shoes, and then took them to the foot of the valet clothes stand, dressed up in the rest of his clothes and looking like a silly scarecrow. He knelt down again to help him on with his pajama pants and then stood up with a heavy sigh seeming to come from somewhere far away; he turned down the covers, settled the boy in the center of the bed, and covered him with a rough sweep of his hand. "So if you want something, you'll call," he told him abruptly, going to the door. Marcos heard his father's footsteps fading down the hallway toward the living room and now, as he lay submerged in the warmth of the covers, the silence started winding its way through the shell of his ears, humming like the sea, and he could feel the solitude he had been longing for begin to take root in his spirit. He swept the room with his eyes, pausing carefully at each object, trying to figure out what hidden common bond there was between so many disparate things. He sensed that the suffocating mishmash of furniture, spread through the rest of the house like heavy underbrush, summed up his father's horror of empty rooms. Landscapes and scenes of Israel, torn from calendars, lined all the walls: the sea of Galilee (or Kineret, as his father knowingly called it), hemmed by a tight ring of hills; a street in Yerushalaim crammed with shops and pedestrians, exactly like Jirón de la Unión Street, right, Marcos? this is the capital of Israel, you wouldn't believe everyone in streets are Jewish, right? blond-dark-redhead and even real black children in a tiny school in Tel Aviv; also the vast wilderness of the Negev with red red sand and where are located the mines King Shlomo, who was very wise; do you know story of two women are fighting for same son and going to King Shlomo . . . ? and also many pictures of Kibbutz Guivat Brenner, founded in year 'twenty-eight, I was one of founders, Marcos, see how beautiful, all people glad working in fields, look how happy everybody, and in fact his father had also worked in the kibbutz, intoning erets zavat chalav, chalav, erets zavat chalav, humming into the wind, land of milk and honey, erets zavat chalav, chalav ud'vash, and in other prints there were young patriarchs, hands twirling the udders of the goats, sinking into the labyrinthine nurseries of the bees . . .

Marcos remembered the first time he had set foot in the house. Startled by the jungle of furniture as he stepped through the door, he stood rooted to the spot; he felt as if all his bones were giving way under a sudden deafening avalanche of rocks. Then his father took his arm and almost dragged him inside toward his room, saying Come, don't be afraid. Left standing alone in his bedroom with his suitcase beside him, he could hardly stay on his feet, a weary taste of rancid almonds in his mouth. From the back of the house his father's voice, as studied as a concierge's, reached him: "This is your room, here you will sleep. Bathroom is a few steps to your left; in front of bathroom is kitchen. You find everything there, unpack your bag, then fix yourself something to eat."

That night, as soon as his mother had gone to her room, the ritual of the bath got under way. "Am going get off all dirt from your body," his father said, rolling up his sleeves with an air of nostalgia for his ancestral past, like an old Orthodox Jew ready to wind the leather maze of phylacteries around his arm. He made Marcos climb into the tub and he let the stream of water out: it came on by fits and starts with a choking sound, then broke out in spurts till it picked up the steady murmur of an easy flow. Steam filled the bathroom with drowsiness, blurred the solid walls, and turned his father into a shadowy figure kneeling next to the tub and already beginning to soap his body with rhythmic skill, as if he were holding a newborn baby, or a body not yet born, molding its form with the nimble fingers of a Florentine goldsmith.

The scene was taking on the importance of a ceremony. The image of baptism in the son's mind corresponded closely to the rites of the biblical patriarch being officiated by his father: an initiation that would take the boy, cleansed of impurities, into his own world. Transformed now into an exterminating angel, his father seemed about to rend his flesh with the pumice stone, a primitive porous knife, without a grip, buried in the depths of his massive fist. The frenzied whirling of his father's hand had all the appearance of an act of martyrdom and Marquitos saw himself being subjected to an ordeal but felt so sure he would come through unharmed that he endured the stabbing stone, held back his tears, and smothered his pain by biting his teeth down hard. Everything else afterward—scrambling out of the tub, scampering to his room, the comforting fetal position under the covers—took place in suspended time, on the hazy verge of sleep.

ONE

: Rushed, Terry slices the ball and it rolls out slowly, wide of the post : Brazil's ball : Gazing toward the edge of the horizon, goalie Gilmar gets ready to kick : and in the West stands, Lima's entire Jewish community leans forward to head the ball :

Everybody is here in our monumental stadium to watch this all-important match : the question in the air is, will Marquitos Karushansky, soccer superstar of Peru and the ancient people of Israel, be able to play? Well, ladies and gentlemen, we must have faith in the healing power of world-famous Dr. Berkowitz, our national team's physician : Here with us at our microphones, Dr. Berkowitz :

> "Marquitos has a very slight inflammation in the urinary tract: Nothing to worry about : only a minor infection brought on by Neisser's gonococcus :

There's a painful secretion of pus from the urethra :

However, there is no need for alarm : a simple operation will do the trick : cutting away the foreskin will make it a lot easier to keep the glans clean :

One week of rest : two shots of penicillin and his penis will be as good as new" :

Brazil's whole forward line spearheads deep into Peru's territory : where a small-town baroque church lies in ruins :

"The 1960 earthquake did it," Marcos's grandfather moves in quickly for the ball :

"It was Satan's work," his grandmother cuts him off and takes control :

"The wrath of God," the voices of the people rise in a long wail that rocks the stands :

Yes, ladies and gentlemen : Marcos has had an extraordinary prophetic dream : and, thanks to the miracle of Peruvian television and to the ever fresh, always delicious Motta fruitcakes, you will have a chance to enjoy it step by step on your screens : And so we see Marcos's dream taking him into a church : In the background we can make out the figure of Christ without His cross : Yes, without His cross : arms dangling at His sides : naked : circumcised : suspended in the air like a battered old rag doll : Kneeling at His feet, an old man with bent head rocks back and forth, chanting a prayer : his thick mane of silver hair glistens : he's coming to his feet now : turning to watch Marcos : does he have grandfather's face? : Father Camacho's? : eyes with a blue gleam in them : an extremely aquiline nose : and a beard that seems out of place on his face : a tangle of strands hanging down to his feet like the branches of a weeping willow :

And here he is now, suddenly stepping to the right as the doors of the temple swing open with a tremendous bang : he pierces Marcos with his eyes, beckons, and the boy comes toward him obediently: Trouble in Peruvian territory : where a grand stairway comes into view at Marcos's feet : the old man takes him by the hand : the two of them go down the steps quietly peering at the road ahead : Suddenly, out of nowhere, the small town comes into sight : The stairway ends inside Marcos's house : the place is deserted and run down : its walls flaking : ceilings caved in : covered with a shroud of cobwebs and dust : The playing field is in terrible shape, fans! : But nothing can hold up this game : They're up to midfield, looking for a way out : going down a passageway crowded with ghosts : they fight their way out, arms flailing, but the Brazilians are marking them very closely : They cross into the penalty zone, a deserted spot, with rubble everywhere : Yes, folks, it's his hometown : only the church is still standing, off there on that hill of sand that looks like ashes : and suddenly the figure of the old man, crouching like a cat, appears outside the church : he motions to Marcos : who makes a desperate run toward him : but the sand gives under the soles of his feet : he falls : and the sand sucks him, head reeling, toward the door of his house : And when he looks up, the hill is gone : only the church is still standing there and in it the old man beckoning once more : But before the boy can react, the old man spins gracefully, turning his back to him, and the doors slam quickly shut : And look at the temple rising into the air, higher, higher, higher! till it soars out of sight and leaves a gray cloud trailing in the sky : like the Peruvian team which has virtually disappeared from the playing field : without our great star Marcos in there, their backs are to the wall, pushed by a powerful Brazilian squad that won't give them any playing room on the field : There's a running commentary from voices all over the stands :

"The Peruvian team is too static :

They'll have to step up the tempo :

They need Marquitos's footwork in midfield :

The sad movement of the *yaraví* can't stay in there with the lively beat of the samba :

We've got to step it up with a *marinera* :

more stomping in the bleachers! :

more drumbeats in the stands! :

They did it once and they can do it again!"

In short, friends, the Peruvian team will have to look for holes deep in enemy territory : On this Saturday afternoon, so ideal for soccer, with a patriotic sellout crowd filling the stadium with waving banners, and our country's honor at stake : injury or no injury, Marquitos cannot and must not be content to stay there, just circling around lovely Manon's asshole : a match Channel 4, always number one on Peruvian television, is happy to broadcast for the entire nation's pleasure, courtesy of CRISTAL, THE CHAMPION OF BEERS :

And now let's watch Marquitos guide his circumcised swollen phallus into Manon's territory : the Peruvian team's advance is too sluggish : And you can tell how upset all of Marquitos's relatives and fellow Jews are at the impotent way the national team is playing : We are very happy to turn over the microphone to our colleague Refugio Cuevas, professor, commentator, and psychologist at León Pinelo School : Take it away, Refugio! :

> "A very good afternoon to you, fellow fans : I'm here on the ground floor to remind you there's no reason to be surprised because home and church haunt Marquitos's dreams at every turn : After all, those are the two worlds that saw him begin to grow and bud into the future unmatched soccer player whose magic talent our team has such a crying need for, this afternoon : What's more, his father Don Yehuda Karushansky is obviously not following field tactics mapped out by the Peruvian coach, venerable Rabbi Goldstein, whose wise counsel, 'a child should receive the tender care of a sapling,' is at the root of the problem : after all, Marquitos's early, premature, violent initiation to a new and peculiar field of play may have brought on psychological problems" :

Our colleague Cuevas is dead right when he says so, just as Marquitos leaps into the fold of the Covenant, like a soul with the Devil breathing down its back : Yes, ladies and gentlemen : at the crack of dawn, father and son trudge slowly up the side of a hill : Yes, it is! : the same hill of ashes that so often haunts poor Marcos in his dreams : The sun works its way through the leaves like a dagger : Where are you taking me, father? Marquitos asks : Don Yehuda doesn't answer : but goes on climbing, never taking his eyes off the top of the hill : his eyes darken : his shadow looks red : fire and wood in his arms : And now Marquitos is on his back on an operating table, the dagger hanging over his eyes : I am a Jew and I also want you be Jew, says Don Yehuda's hollow voice : Did you say Jew? : Yes, Jew! : Jew for Peruvians but Yid among us, you hear? :

There's no getting around it! : Our colleague Cuevas was right : Señor Karushansky is just screwing up the progress of this match : Instead of organizing plays, he's cramping our teamwork : And there's no one to pull this one out for us : What we need this afternoon is for Rabbi Goldstein, seated on Señor Karushansky's right, to turn to his God for the help our team needs : and to rock with his soulful prayer the foundations of our enormous synagogue that is now too small to hold our numerous fans :

"Baruch atah Adonai :
Eloheinu melech ha-olam :
asher kidshanu . . . :
And so on :

Five minutes into the first half and Brazil has the ball : A short push-pass from Didí to Vavá : he spins the ball with his left boot and moves upfield with his eye on his forwards who are fanning out : Manon spreads out her perfumed petals : but Marquitos will have no part of this, because what's on his mind now is how to get away from his father's constant harassment and save our great country from defeat : from being swept off the field : and it hurts me to say this, fellow Peruvians, but Peru is gradually being swept, echad shtayim shalosh, out of Marquitos's life : He's already forgetting its geography and its history : And if not, let him tell us who León Pinelo was : not to be confused in any way with our great national hero Leoncio Prado : who, fighting to save his country from vile treason, unfurls Israel's blue-and-white flag and plunges into the sea with the invading horde of Philistines, I mean Chileans, in hot pursuit : And all of us Peruvians drink INKA KOLA : THE PERUVIAN DRINK OF QUALITY : And don't forget : if you're looking for a good school for your children, send them to León Pinelo : we guarantee they'll learn to be one-hundred-percent Peruvian there : like Atahualpa who was never brought to his knees and was proud to be Jewish and happy at the same time : Jewish? : A goddamn lie! : Hey, who said so? : Let him show his face on the screen so we can all see who it is! :

Yes! there he is in the stands, it's the rabbi, crouching in his seat, as Zagalo flies like a deer into the forest of the Peruvian area : He feeds a short ball to Vavá who fires it right back like a bullet : Zagalo wheels and shoots a cannonball to starboard! and loose-limbed Zegarra, covering the far corner of the net, makes a last-minute save :

Moments of pressure on Peru's backfield and in the stands, tremendous nervous tension among the Jews on this splendid sunny afternoon : while quivering sunbeams filter through the venetian blinds and throw light on the vaguely seen contours of Manon's body : next to her Marquitos, his strength sapped by the gonococcus, follows the action step by step : There goes a high lob carrying danger toward the right-hand corner : Garrincha races for the ball : close on his tail, the Leoncio Prado physician, Dr. Belisario Márquez, an excellent fullback : he stretches his bow : Garrincha feints from right to left and the arrow flies straight for the team bench where it sinks into Marquitos's body : a critical, deadly injury : O Adonai Eloheinu, please don't let him die on us! Adonai Eloheinu melech ha-olam Who art in heaven killing buzzards!

Here's the eminent Dr. Berkowitz with us once more, to explain in simple language the nature of the injury Marquitos suffered playing against Uruguay :

> "So far, we have not been able to stop the infection from spreading : Without skin to protect it, the glans tends to grow coarser and less sensitive, and this delays orgasm and ejaculation : After a week, a chancre shows up : a hard egg-shaped erosion : Then all the body's tissues are infected through the bloodstream : the skin turns paler gradually and necrotic brown spots appear : The areas of growth and roots start to die : scarlet internal tissues show through the fleshy parts of the stem as it begins to deteriorate : The infection produces roseola :
> mucuslike secretions :
> fatigue :
> headaches :
> mental disturbances :
> insanity :
> and even general paralysis" :

Yes, folks : Marquitos is going to die! : death stalks him at midfield : kansaywan wañuyka kuskam kusham purin! : Life and death, said the Indian sages in the old days, always walk hand in hand! : He knows he's going to die, and we know it too : Even penicillin or tetramycin can't help now : He's going to die on a rainy day : and he'll be buried in Peruvian ground where this history-making contest is on right now : Take a good look at him : he's breathing much too fast : an infection zigzagging through his body is eating him up : it's spreading through the bloodstream : it's latching on to his nerve tissues like a buzzard's claws : Danger! : soaring fever, cramps : it's attacking pelvis, heart, testicles : And that's why, at night, when all the other cadets in his section are sound asleep, Marcos jerks off very quietly under the Leoncio Prado Academy blanket, trying to dump out the infection : Look out! : there goes a hot fast shot! it smashes into the post and caroms out : the Peruvian goalie's ball : Yes, yes, friends : Oh there are deaths and O deaths! : But who will shed tears for him when he's gone! : No one! : Not even his father : who is nowhere in sight at this moment that's so excruciating for Peru :

What does lady luck hold in store for Peru? : That's the million-dollar question that worries, crucifies, and burns in the flesh of one and every sports fan in this great nation : Injured in dangerous play with Manon, the whore, Marquitos Karushansky Ávila is not on the playing field : And Peru, friends, needs him there :

The million-dollar question : would Marquitos, injury and all, play for Israel's team? : It's painful, but true : in this fantastic tournament Peru has lost one of its glorious vassals : the pride and glory of adoring parents : two races merging in a historic and harmonious union to create the new Peruvian man : Marquitos Karushansky Ávila, your country needs you! :

And there he is, fans, on your home screens : deep in thought, daydreaming about his Hebraic-Indian ancestry while Manon lovingly fondles his prick and he waits for Peru's coach to tell him : C'mon, Marquitos, get out there and play ball! : It's all up to you to save Peru! : And don't say beer : say CRISTAL : THE CHAMPION OF BEERS :

TWO

That's right: in those days the school stood where the new synagogue is now. After all these years, it's almost impossible to still have a clear picture of it, see?

Yeah, but I remember it as being a flat, uninterrupted white (maybe on the creamy side) and taking up half an ordinary block between General Garzón and Brazil Avenue (the streetcars to La Punta still used that route then).

Yes, on the edge of town, where Pueblo Libre starts, not quite developed at that end of Lima. There were empty lots, more like garbage dumps; a scattering of houses, shacks made of cardboard and straw; tough-looking mulatto kids kicking the ball around or using rocks to play target practice with dirty, rawboned dogs drifting around in packs.

Right. A pretty dreary dump, out in the middle of nowhere, with all kinds of wild trees whose names we didn't even know, wind and dustclouds, we never went out there.

What for? We didn't have to. Well, maybe we were scared to go out there alone. We weren't used to doing anything like that. We were mama's boys, always hanging on to mama's hand on the way to school and back home again.

But Cholo Marcos had been there, at least it's what he said. He didn't have a mama to take him to school by the hand. And he wasn't afraid, he said, to wander down Lima's Bolívar. He used to walk all the way to the old Indian cemetery, he wasn't scared, there was one just like it outside his hometown.

Pueblo Libre is not Lima, he used to say. It had orchards and streams and farms. Yeah, that's right, on the other side of Brazil Avenue.

The school entrance was on Húsares de Junín. You'd walk right by without noticing it; it was more like a rathole than a doorway. Not like afterward, now, at the new school they built later on Orrantia.

No, nobody was really trying to hide. We're talking to you about a different time: years of transition, when the Community was just starting to get on its feet. We were, I mean our parents were going through what they call the fat years. The right winds were blowing. From door-to-door rag dealers they had gone on to become big wholesalers, and those not so well off at least had their own little store.

Yes, favorable winds were blowing and things were picking up, but why stick your neck out, huh? Besides, there wasn't a private school in Lima without high walls around it, so we weren't the only ones . . .

León Pinelo School? No, it didn't have much of a name in those days. They had bought the site recently (some people say the first school, on Breña, had been an old viceroy's palace).

Well, there was a Community drive. Everyone—our parents used to puff up when they talked about it—chipped in their little donation and they were able to move the school. It would have made an ideal convent: the classrooms had no windows and were more like cells, lined up in a row opposite the soccer field. During gym class we had to play bunched up close to the back wall, in a very narrow space that took up only about a third of the whole field.

And if anybody yelled, or puffed too heavily, or so much as sneezed, whack! he got cuffed on the head. Yeah, the professor fixed us all right; the bastard used to hit real hard with the stone on his ring, a sharp rap. We played in sneakers, and all you could hear was the ball bouncing, hitting the posts, or its impact on our shoes as we kicked it . . . :

Sure, I guess the neighborhood knew about it, or at least had to know it was a school, but I'm not sure they knew its name or that it was Jewish. Anyhow, since the back wall faced several houses, they must have soon found out, no?

I remember they used to spy on us from behind their windows. It was like part of a prearranged ritual we had learned to expect, but that didn't make it less terrifying. They did their best to keep out of sight and that was part of the mystery, the terror nobody ever talked about.

They had apparently memorized our schedule. When we went out into the yard for recess, they were right there on the upper floors, their eyes fastened on us. At one point, we even thought maybe it was a nut house.

And that's not everything, all the inmates were deaf-mutes, not a single word ever came from the other side of the wall . And with the racket we kicked up during recess, living on the other side must have been hell, don't you think?

Still, nobody on the other side ever complained.

But there was one son-of-a-bitch who had a way of getting even with us. When we played soccer, if a ball flew over the wall, it was sure to come back with all the air let out of it.

Ah, but that wasn't all, letting the air out was one thing but what this character did was something else again. He slashed it up good. With its rubber insides pouring out, it looked like a skinned cat with its guts sticking out; he had us all scared stiff. And we could never get used to this, we were afraid he might hurdle the wall any day and make minced meat of us.

Was he anti-Semitic? No, we really don't know. I personally believe the guy was just plain crazy.

If I'd been him, I wouldn't have returned those balls.

You? You bet your life you wouldn't have! This smart-ass would've opened a sporting-goods store and taken business away from Tito Drago.

Sure, we can be smug and laugh about it now, but we were shitting in our pants then. We were still wet behind the ears, in second grade, with knee-pants and all. And the only one of us who wasn't afraid was Cholo (it was our pet name for Marcos, see).

But all this was only at the start, when he first came to the school, during the first two or three games. School had just opened and we hadn't lost a ball yet. We were playing one day; the ball dropped on the other side and Cholo says to us give me a boost, he was going to climb over right now and retrieve the ball.

We had to tell him not to be a schmuck, they'd slit him open if he went over. Besides, who was going to help him get back to our side? So he said we were a bunch of fairies, it was our fault the game was over. Jeesus, he sure liked to play soccer! It was like he was addicted to it.

You guys remember the first time? First day of school: we were kicking the ball around and Cholo was sitting on the ground watching us out of the corner of his eye like he couldn't care less but never taking his eyes off us. We asked if he wanted to come in the game, we were one player short. We didn't have to ask a second time! He started taking his shoes off right away, and then his socks.

And us huddled together gaping at him, it was all we could do to keep from laughing. And him, remember? with his countrified accent, bluffing but also kind of shy, What's your problem, why were we laughing like that.

Well, he wasn't even embarrassed. He didn't want his shoes to get dirty, what was wrong with that? He stood there, looking like he was spoiling for a fight, hands on hips, standing his ground, and us (not that we were afraid, we could have ganged up on him and knocked the piss out of him), don't be silly, we were going to play on cement, didn't he know he'd get blisters under his feet?

What all didn't we tell him! No use, because him, Don't worry about what I'm doin', c'mon, what side am I on? Honestly, he didn't look at all like a soccer player: all skin and bones, knees like doorknobs, real sorry-looking—but what a whiz with the ball! He left us sprawled all over the place: a feint this way, that way, moving around the field like he was in his own front parlor. An absolute master with the ball, he took it up and down the field like it was glued to his foot, dribbling most of us, cocky, making fun of us, Here's the ball, come and get it. Who was gonna get it away from him! To do it we'd've had to foul him and even that didn't always work.

No, he didn't play barefoot anymore, but he still insisted it was much better. It was easier to spin the sphere (I'm not putting you on, it's exactly how he talked), push the orb gently, coax the pigskin, and a helluva lot more soccer talk.

Besides, he was right at home with it. He had played on cobblestone streets in his hometown: Hey, in his town everybody played barefoot, hey, Lima's full of fairies. Yeah, he talked a lot about his town.

But only at first, right?, because he buttoned up later on.

Right, he became more reserved as time went on. Hard to say when it started and at first we may not even have noticed the change in him. His hometown? I don't even know. Any of you guys remember what it was called?

I believe he was always changing its name. And

not only its name but also where it was on the map. What a fucking guy, he used to put us on like nobody's business. And now I laugh my head off when I think what a big joke it was, hearing him talk about the climate there. Listen to this: the place was somewhere where it snowed, rained, and was blistering hot, all on the same day. You'd wake up and it was snowing. The flakes, he swore on his mother's grave (sometimes he even seemed about to bless himself but stopped in the nick of time), the snowflakes were the shape and size of a guava and floated down on the town like a slow swarm of white feathers...

It snowed till noon more or less, right? And then the sun we mentioned before, a savage jungle sun, would suddenly beat down hard. By then everybody in town had locked their doors and windows, because the sun's glare on the snow was so blinding they all stayed in, afraid to lose their sight. Isn't that something?

Well, it happened to one of his aunts who (so Marcos said) was half cracked. One day, before anybody could stop her, she rushed out into the street and hadn't gone more'n a couple of steps before the sun turned her whole body as white as the snow.

Marcos said the family could only look at her through a small crack in the door. The old woman had gone completely blind; suddenly, she stretched out her arms and started spinning around like a top, and then went down the street spinning like that, ramming into the walls of houses, till they lost sight of her. Nobody ever knew for sure what became of her.

At least we didn't, because Cholo never finished

any of his stories. I don't know how he managed to get away with it, but he always left us guessing, like when he came up with the tall one about some other aunt and the mirrors...

Or about the uncle who went to the top of a hill (the cops were waiting for him below with guns) to paint the APRA initials in gigantic letters.

Or his grandfather who used to store away the butter in his strongbox so the rest of the family wouldn't steal it... And another uncle eloped with a trapeze artist who had come to town with a circus, and so on.

In fact, it was hard to believe anything he said, so we used to give him a hard time.

We were actually just trying to get back at him, and each time he popped up with one of his tall stories we made him swear, remember?

Cholo was forever coming up with some super-Catholic crap. He'd touch his crossed thumb and forefinger to his lips, kiss them, let out a kind of sucking sound and swear up and down in the name of Our Lady of the Door or the Cave... or some other Virgin! And us, like real pricks, no, not like that, he had to swear the Jewish way. C'mon, swear it's true! I swear to God who is my shining light! : What? : To God! : No, not like that, do it right. Chai Adonai! Chai Adonai! Cholo would say, perfectly embarrassed.

But don't think we had it in for him, no sir, just the opposite, we really liked him, and since he was so good at soccer, we respected and admired him. He told us how we should play, how to dribble, head the ball, aim it at the far corner of the net. He also told us where to position ourselves on the field and how to fan out . . . :

We always listened to him because Cholo obviously knew all about those things—and when we lost a championship game, he'd get bitter and tell us off in front of our parents, but he'd soon get over it. No use crying over it, he'd say, we'll make it the next time. And we never squawked, because we felt sorry for him. His mother had died, he told us, but what they were saying in the Community was she'd gone back home, and that there had even been a big row, right?

Yes, apparently it was quite a scandal, with threats of murder, jail, and everything. We don't actually know how much of all this was true. Yeah, he was still living over on Jesús María then, but later he and his old man relocated to Breña.

His house? I don't remember it. If I'm not wrong, we were there only once, no? He seemed to be embarrassed about something there, because he would never ask us to his house. He wasn't like us, I mean his life wasn't like ours. For instance, any of you remember being at his Bar Mitzvah?

All I recall is he was preparing for it. On Saturdays he went to the house of a weird little old man they said had been a rabbi in the Community in the old days: he taught him the prayers and they probably practiced his speech together. Yeah, all Bar Mitzvah speeches were more or less the same. Dear parents, relatives, and friends: I'd like to thank you for coming to celebrate with me this day of vital importance in my life. It marks my initiation as a member of the Congregation of Israel. As a Jew and disciple of Moses, from now on I am responsible for all my acts, and so I must work hard to stay on the road to perfection. And on this day of special significance to me, I raise my voice in prayer to our Father in heaven, may He guide me toward truth and justice as a good Jew, and so on, right?

Yes, we all had to go through the same mill. But I'm almost sure there was no ceremony or party for Marcos. As a matter of fact, we didn't receive an invitation, so who knows if he ever even had a Bar Mitzvah. But it was always the same with him—he wasn't like the rest of us. No, he wasn't an exception, except maybe for our generation.

Because Marcos was the first to appear out of nowhere. All of us here had grown up together. Together we went through nursery, kindergarten, and grade school. And we all saw one another at Betar. Then one day Cholo drops in out of the blue—we didn't even dream there could be Jews in the sticks. But later, in fourth or fifth grade, when the lid came off, they started to pour in like... like a plague of locusts, right?

But none as weird as Cholo—like the bit about his circumcision, right?

Exactly, and even now we're still not sure just what happened. The only one who knew about it, besides him, were his old man and the doctor who did the operation.

It's a pity Jaime Ackerman isn't with us now, because he started the whole thing. We were in second grade and one day, during recess, Jaime came over and pulled us aside, he had a secret. He had just come from the toilet and, you won't believe this, guess what I just saw. And us, go on, let's have it. And Jaime, Cholo hadn't had a bris: What d'ya mean he hasn't had a bris! You sure? And Jaime Yes, very sure. He was taking a leak next to Cholo and he saw there was a hood on his pecker. He was positive! Cholo hadn't had a bris!

And at this point Cholo suddenly showed up. Hell, we could hardly keep still! We faked it, Where ya bin, brother? But he must've smelled something, because he stood there giving Jaime a funny look. Lucky for us the bell rang and we all made a dash for the classroom. He sauntered in a little later with a face that said There's something rotten here, remember?

Yeah, but how could he know we were in on his secret?

I don't know how, but he did, because from then on, remember? he would never go to the toilet when any of us did. If he had to take a leak, he waited for the bell, he ran there like a bat out of hell, pissed real fast, and came flying back to the classroom. But we wanted to make sure and used to trail him to the bathroom and never used to leave the poor guy alone. We didn't do it to be mean, it was only curiosity—we'd never seen a pecker with a hood before.

But that's not the whole story—because whenever we went to the machaneh, Cholo wouldn't strip in front of us either. Yeah, let me explain: Every year when vacation came around we Betar Club members used to go camping near Chosica. We slept in tents and in the middle of camp we set up a pole with the flags of Peru and Israel at the top, just like pioneers in those kibbutzim on the Israeli border, right?

Well, not quite...

Anyway, we stayed there three, maybe four weeks living like real pioneers. We had to fetch water from the river every day, cook, clean up camp, and we even had people stand guard at night. The kids our age shared one tent. We bathed in a pool that Cholo, out playing the explorer, had discovered in the river and given the name Alligator Lagoon. But he'd never change his clothes with us; sometimes he put his trousers on over his swim trunks and had a wet ass all day long because he was afraid to let us see him naked.

Then one summer, one or two weeks before leaving for the machaneh, we heard that he'd been circumcised. Cholo was our age, twelve at the time. Yeah, he went to the machaneh but during the three weeks we spent there, we didn't get to see him naked even once. He wouldn't change or else did it behind some bushes near our tent. So we figured all that stuff about his circumcision had been a false alarm. Naturally we didn't ask him, so as not to embarrass him. And when we went back to school it went right on. Cholo kept up the same old tricks so we wouldn't see his pecker. No, we never faced him with it, not even when we found out he was going to Israel...

Yes, going to Israel had always been his one big dream—but that was a lot later, in 1963. We all went down to the pier to say goodbye. He was happy as a lark. No, he left and never even dropped us a line. We had no news of him till 1967, when the war broke out, remember?

How could we forget it? It was a lightning war, like something right out of the Bible... and all the Lima Community couldn't have been more delighted when the newspapers said little David had brought down the giant Goliath with a well-placed stone, or else Judas Maccabeus, battle hammer in hand, had put to flight the army of King Antiochus.

And so it was. In just six days, victorious Israeli troops marched to the gates of Egypt. You can imagine all the excitement! The whole Community was decked out with decorations and we celebrated the victory on every street corner. Ah, it was different being a Jew now—that week, all of us, grownups and kids, strutted around, didn't we? heads high, remembering Jabotinsky's famous words, I cannot bow my head, for God has made me straight!

In the middle of the celebrations, the news hit us: Marcos had been killed in action. A bullet went right through him, some people said, and others, it was a bayonet. And there was no one around to ask about it because by 1967 his father was dead... (in circumstances we won't go into now). But with Marcos's death (or as you say, his reported death) we saw the war in a different light. It got closer to us; it sneaked in under our doors and we could sniff the smell of gunpowder in our homes...

Where did the rumor of his death get started? No one ever found out, but apparently it caught fire in several places at the same time. Why? Because the Community thrived on myths (and still does) ... who knows? Maybe we needed a local hero, and we picked Marcos...

There (or so we thought then), in a remote

corner of the Sinai, his story had come to an end... But now you come telling us Cholo didn't die in the war. You come telling us, as if it's nothing, that he blew his brains out... How can you expect us to believe it! Huh?

THREE

: The Peruvian team is now crossing midfield : Rabbit Benítez has the ball : he fires it to Joya : Zózimo comes out to mark him : he challenges him at the midfield circle : sizes him up : sniffs : Manon catches his cock with her lips : covered with spit the delicious glob slides toward the isthmus of her throat : Zózimo sticks his foot in hard and takes the ball away from him: a complex move that involves a number of reflexes : the excitement encourages a coordinated rhythm : Zózimo gives to Garrincha : who quickly breaks away up the right side : he gets set to center the ball : her tongue gropes upward : her epiglottis closes around Peruvian territory : The ball floats in an arc looking for the goalmouth : her larynx moves up closer : Pelé leaps into the air : he heads the ball just over the line of defenders and the glob grazes the bar on its way out :

Trouble again for the goal defended by Zegarra : USE KOLYNOS AND SMILE : KOLYNOS, THE SUCCESSFUL MAN'S TOOTHPASTE :

Fifteen minutes of play and the scoreboard still registers 0 to 0 : we don't know or even try to guess what lady luck has in store for the great Marquitos, still warming the bench, lulled there in the arms of Manon the enchantress : Will they kick him out of the Leoncio Prado Military Academy? :

This question runs like wildfire through all the stands, while Marquitos waits for instructions from Coach Muñoz so as to sneak over to the bunk of Cadet Aranzani, a real cutie with his Sandra Dee babyface, and in the nocturnal silence of the Tenth Section, Fifth Year barracks, drives in a fantastic one-shot goal : GOAL . . . ! Goal scored by Pelé eighteen minutes into the first half : a ball that slipped into the far corner where spiders spin their nets :

What a dash of cold water this goal is : Well, let's see if the defense can tighten up its ass and not let another shot get through it : No sign of Marquitos yet! : Folks, Peru could not have reached these finals against Brazil without his brilliant playing : he's putting his exceptional skills to work right now in the room of Manon the big whore : there she is now, on your screens, in front of her mirror : She dips her hips and shoulders, feinting coyly : stands on tiptoe : her heels light on the floor gracefully : she pirouettes with the delicate movements of a ballet dancer : her tiny mouth puckers as if to suck Marquitos's cock : she has bland fleshy lips made to order for the boy's member : Manon can hardly wait for Marquitos to come out of school : racing across the field in his flashy uniform to her room for the usual Saturday service : Everybody knows it : on Shabbat, a holy day for all our people, the Jewish community calls all its members together : North and South : East and West : to our stadium : to celebrate at least one Bar Mitzvah : a ceremony Channel 4, ever ready to observe our country's traditions, is happy to bring into every home in Peru :

After a long pilgrimage from San Isidro to Jesús María, a capacity crowd is squeezing into the synagogue : they're packed in like sardines : the tickets for this thrilling event have been sold out for days : Scalpers in the streets are trying to cash in on it : But admission is by invitation only and now everyone is greeting pouter-pigeon mama who is wearing her finest jewels and her sweetest Viennese smile : and there is papa, more skin than bones, exuding happiness through every pore in his long-suffering body : and the young Bar Mitzvah kid, with his plump little ass, who in a few minutes, by divine grace of Adonai, will come off the bench to join the stars of the undefeated team of the Covenant :

Father and son cross the half-moon and approach the bimah : The rabbi comes in like a shadow from the right wing : he blows his whistle and the game gets under way : In the synagogue his powerful voice shakes the ark, the bulb of the eternal light, the small mahogany lions holding up the Tablets, and the overflowing hearts of the entire Jewish community, while the prayers to the Father, the Son, and the Holy Ghost amen bounce, crisscrossing, from wall to wall like cosmic rays : Waiters single-file in swiftly with the food and the distinguished guests rush around from table to table like happy flies, and the young Bar Mitzvah stands up to make his speech in a chanting voice filled with emotion :

"I feel that today marks the beginning of my coming of age and I want to express my admiration and my love for my dear parents, who have always been my spiritual guides," and indeed, here is some nourishing chicken soup now : "And therefore I promise to grow up to be a good man and always keep in mind the short phrase packed with so much meaning" : appetizing latkes, eye-filling gefilte fish : "Kabed vetikabed : Honor your neighbor that you may be honored" : and in the background, some seviche, so Peruvian, camouflaged but never hidden, mouth-watering and always a good fill-in : "And one last word : this moment will be engraved with an undying flame deep within me : because my true mission in life begins today : To be a Jew" : Wow, are these chili peppers hot! : But they are real Peruvians and their eyes don't water : However, tears run freely down mama's round cheeks : as she sees her son growing into quite a little man : "But it's not easy being a Jew : For me being a Jew is to obey my parents in everything : and to obey in everything that Moshe Rabeinu has taught us is our heritage : and to help build Medinat Israel" : while a committee of ladies takes up the usual collection for Keren Kayemet Leisrael, and draws a generous contribution of tears : "And when anyone asks who I am, I shall proudly say : I'M A JEW!" : A wild ovation in the stands : people laugh happily : sing : dance : To a waltz! a *marinera*! : a *tonderito*! : And to please everyone, a couple of Israeli dances : Tzena tzena tzena tzena : avara turena chayali : lamoshavah : ah : ah : ah : and jumuq wata in Yerushalaim! :

But the linesman is raising his red-and-white flag and the referee calls a foul in favor of Peru : The players of the Jewish team protest the call and hell breaks loose on the field : The rabbi is obviously letting the game slip through his fingers : Here with us once more, our colleague Refugio Cuevas : Take it away, Refugio! :

> Ladies and gentlemen, it's time to come right out with it : Our country's honor is at stake : Are we going to let Marquitos defect to the other side just because of his authoritarian father's whim? I say no! : And you, fellow Peruvians, should do the same : cry out to the Almighty God and demand our inalienable right to be Peruvians and to be proud of it : even if we, like Marquitos, have :
> a brachycephalic skull :
> legs much too short for our bodies :
> a long broad chest :
> straight coarse hair :
> prominent cheekbones :
> and semi-Mongoloid eyes :
> Remember : what really counts is not the flesh but the soul :
> And we are a patient race : stoic : sensitive : moody : and sad :

That's saying it, Cuevas, my friend! : And we want to make it plain that our immortal Marquitos is not to blame for any of this, he has clearly proved, time and again, that he is a Peruvian through and through : Then why are those Fifth Year cadets taking him to the latrine ? : Watch out! fans : There are three of them and they have him trapped : The one in front arches his eyebrows, sizing him up : He can't see the faces of the other two : they flank him and brace themselves against the wall : He can only hear them breathing : loud, hot blasts that sting his eyes : They're marking him more tightly now : A sharp burning itch runs through his body as if it were covered with prickly heat : but he stands his ground with his hands digging hard into his thighs : his ears are buzzing because he's dead scared : He looks out the corner of his eye at the door as if half expecting someone or something to come in : but the whole school is asleep : only the sea's guttural even purr drifts in : The one facing him raises his fist : Marcos shifts out of the way : he opens his eyes and sees a different fist there : he ducks : The others burst out laughing : the one on his right lets him have it on the head : "Faggot Dog! Hey, look at him, we haven't started in yet and he's already crapping in his pants" : Marcos stays doubled up : his eyes burn : tears are welling up but he fights them back, gritting his teeth : And the Fifth Year man, in a high-pitched voice : "Stand up, you shit!" And then the others again : "He looks like a scared little whore, don't he?" : The joke draws a horselaugh from all three : Marcos has straightened up : he leans against the wall : The Fifth Year men order him : "Stay put, damn it!" : They go into a huddle a few steps away and start whispering : then they come over to him again, shoulders thrown back, a hard grin on their faces : "Dog, we want you to be a good Leoncio Prado cadet and do us a favor" : The tallest, the one with the high voice, steps up to him : "The three of us have made a bet and you're to decide who's the winner : Now snap to, chest out good and high" : Marcos obeys : he swells his chest all he can : The shortest one moves in and wham! nails him with his fist : Marcos feels himself thrown against the wall and pain spreads through him like splintered glass : They tell him to brace up again and this time the powerhouse comes from the fat one : He bounces off the wall and the third one is waiting, ready : wham! : a sharp blow, his head hits the wall : his knees start to buckle but he fights to stay on his feet : "C'mon, Dog, which of us three throws the hardest punch?" : Marcos doesn't answer : they push him around : "Tell us who won the bet!" At last Marcos says that all three hit just as hard : "Then it means we have to break the deadlock!" : "Snap to!" : "Get away from the wall, damn it!" : Everything around him goes black, at the first blow : then there is the second : and the third : Marcos isn't sure anymore where the blows are coming from : then he thinks about his father, who also beats him : his father goes wild with rage sometimes and pounds him hard with his fists : only to feel sorry afterward and break out crying : "Marcos, is for own good" that he does it : "your studies before everything else," and brings up his friends at the León Pinelo : "Why can't you be like them?" : They study hard, those with high grades, who grab all the prizes at the end of the year : "Is my duty to guide you along right path" and the old man's eyes water . . . :

But Marcos is not going to cry : "Answer, Dog! which of us hits the hardest?" : And the whirling arms spin him around and around like he was rolling downhill while something fights hard to break out of his throat : Something that has to do with his mother, something that rolls into an angry lump in his chest : "Answer, damn it!" : But it's easier not to answer : to shut his eyes and concentrate on a fixed point he sees deep inside himself : Everything's reeling : something burns him, something in his brain : He feels his legs giving and he starts to collapse very slowly. . . : A foul the referee signals in favor of the Brazilian team! :

Didí kicks the foul : short, over to Pelé : he dribbles an opponent, shoots with his left, and : Second goal for Brazil, ladies and gentlemen : The scoreboard now shows 2 to 0 in its team's favor : Believe it or not, the Peruvian defense is a shambles! : Our great country needs Marquitos : whose father doesn't even suspect that, on this day of glorious sunshine, they are about to expel his son from Leoncio Prado Military Academy : Marquitos Karushansky Ávila : accused of fucking Cadet Aranzani up the ass in the barracks of Section Ten, Fifth Year : Marquitos Karushansky Ávila : The biggest asshole reamer in Lima! : who—according to the grapevine —was spotted celebrating the traditional feast of Purim at the masquerade ball at Laguna de Barranco : And indeed, dear fans, on your screens you can see this Sodom and Gomorrah of masked balls, bringing disgrace upon the Jewish community of Lima : The mayor of Miraflores is now making his grand entrance, dressed as a Creole Madame Pompadour : a platinum-blond chignon, pointed slippers that have tassels strung with jewels, a beauty spot on his left cheek, and fine perfumed face powder : Others come dressed in hooded cloaks or as harlequins, Pierrots and peg-legged pirates with an eyepatch : Among the ladies we can make out Colombines in fantastic dresses made of percale and velvet and eighteenth-century perukes : A chamber-music orchestra adds a special touch to this ball which includes a number of adolescents evidently brought to this magnificent carnival party against their will, after being given drugs whose effects have not been detected by the medic on duty, Dr. Belisario Márquez of the Leoncio Prado school staff : Yes folks : we're all here at the Laguna, selected for this Purim celebration because of the romantic atmosphere prevalent here : moonlight flooding the lake, boat rides through the tunnel of love, and above all, charming cabañas on the west bank of the lake, where couples may retire to recover from the wear and tear of the dance : And we've just heard that they've hustled a teenager, barely sixteen years old, into one of the cabañas : we cannot give out his name and address until an investigation has been made by Lieutenant Montenegro who will see to it that Leoncio Prado is not overrun by a bunch of faggots :

Leoncio Prado Cadets :
Set your sights high : like our banner :
Let your spirit glow : like a flame :
And be stout-hearted : an honor
To the man who gave our school his name :

But anyone can see Marquitos doesn't give a damn : Hidden in their Section Ten quarters with

Cadet Aranzani, Marquitos is only conscious of the pounding in his heart : His eyes hunt for Cadet Aranzani, a real cutie with his Sandra Dee babyface : A Lima Gidget parading her girlish charms on the golden sands of La Herradura beach :

And so it is that Sandra, virginal and pure as the driven snow, declares her love for Cadet Karushansky : her unblemished teenage love : for Sandra, reticent daughter of a good Miraflores family, is not a common whore : Then why doesn't she protest, moan, or cry when Cadet Vega, the big bully, a weightlifter, rams it into her in bed at night? :

The Peruvian defense has its back to the wall : Vega creeps into Aranzani's bunk : he pulls down his pajama bottom : not a word from Sandra : he lifts his rosy ass a little, in a kind of parabola, and Cadet Karushansky almost passes out playing with himself : ball that rolls out wide of the net, and it's a goal kick for Peru :

FOUR

The academy was in La Perla, right on Costanera Avenue. Hugging the coast, almost hanging over the edge of the cliff, right?

Yes, on the cliff's edge, some seventy feet away, maybe less, on the other side of the highway. A huge block of cement, solid, yellow and gray, walls on all four sides. We called it Sing-Sing, remember?

Right. And not very far off, farther down Costanera, was its twin.

The reform school! We could see it from the bus on the way home, Saturdays. It was the spittin' image of our school, walled in, gray. Its entrance, an enormous iron gate with very thick bars...

In winter, the school looked like a ghost town at night—floating there, draped in mist. And the sea seeping into everything; it peeled the paint from walls, bunks, lockers.

Everything gave off a smell of sulfur, the way I remember it. Sometimes a nauseating stench came up the cliff, like rotting fish, leftovers. They must have been using the whole area as a sewer and we got most of the stink.

When you got there, the place made you feel as if you'd just stepped off a long trip, as if you had landed suddenly, without any warning, in another world that had nothing to do with ours.

And yet all of us lived in Lima, a half-hour's bus ride from there. So you can figure out what it was like for those who came from somewhere else, from the mountains, or from the Amazon jungle. It must have been like landing on another planet, see?

We were little runts no taller'n this, when we first came there in Third Year, and the school looked to us more like a small village. I'm not putting you on—seven blocks long and some two blocks wide. It had everything you can think of: mess halls, barracks, offices; classrooms, infirmary, swimming pool; chapel, barber shop, canteen, and what not . . .

Tailor shop, stadium. If we wanted to play soccer, basketball—we had nine, ten playing fields. There was even a printing press, and a general headquarters behind the stadium.

Yeah, it was just like a village. Little plazas all over the place, with their own street lamps and benches, just like in any neighborhood in Lima. You walked around the school grounds and, believe it or not, it was like being out in the street.

Sure. The parade ground was as wide as an avenue. It ran the whole length of the school, end to end. And there was the main building . . .

From a terrace there, the Colonel would spout his endless speeches. The big brass were always coming up with some kind of ceremony: Independence Day, Army Day, the anniversary of Leoncio Prado's death, his birth—anything they could think of.

We'd be lined up in front of him, looking real sharp. Anyone who so much as budged one inch went on report. Restricted Saturday and Sunday! And if he didn't like it, he could take it up with the pope.

Yes, the main building was the heart of the school, the head of the octopus. The Colonel's office was there. The whole building was a web of offices, never-ending, dark marble passageways. It was like a mausoleum, cold, creepy.

No, we almost never went in there. We didn't dare, not with so many officers prowling around at every turn. We'd go right past, scared stiff, in military step, chest out, head high, just in case.

Still, the Goats and the Cows had us even more terrified. Yes, the cadets in Fifth and Fourth. We're talking about when we were Dogs, in Third. The Cows and the Goats seemed a lot older than us, a lot bigger, already starting to grow fuzz. And naturally they were always giving us a rough time.

We had to salute them all the time, any place. And if we goofed off and went by without doing it, they made us pull up right there, Halt! Trying to play dumb, hey? They would force us to walk back a whole block and march past again, a little more respect, damn it! Then we outdid ourselves saluting, scared to death, stiff, not batting an eyelid.

It was even worse when they marched us off to their barracks at night to make their bunks. What could we do! Nothing! Obey orders, let them treat us like nice little Dogs.

But that wasn't the worst part, eh? Saluting, making beds. Because the sons-of-bitches had a thousand ways to fuck us up. Remember what they used to do to us in the toilet? Get a load of this. We would be there in the latrine after lunch, taking a quiet shit, when a Cow or a Goat—it made no difference—would suddenly pop in, somebody would shout, 'tenshun! and all of us in Third, trousers dropped to our ankles, would have to jump to attention. Remember? On the spot.

How can we forget it! Anybody who moved, so much as a hair, got fifteen, twenty pushups with his hands braced against the bowl. And of course they wouldn't even let us pull the chain... No, that was the best part of the fun! To leave the bowl brimming with shit. And then make us do twenty, maybe thirty pushups in a row, inhaling deep and liking it.

Gripe? Hell no! That would have made us fairies. On the first day, they made it very clear to us. Men never beef! Beef? No sir. We'd have to be crazy. Go complain to a captain or a lieutenant? Not on your life. First off, they wouldn't have listened to us, and second, we'd be laying ourselves wide open for those in Fifth and Fourth to bear down on us hard. And then school would have been hell on earth.

Okay, it's exactly what happened to the Jew, remember? Yes, we're talking about Karushansky. Jew? We called him that because we liked him, don't think it was otherwise... Let me go on. The guys in Fifth and Fourth came down on him with a vengeance. Well, they picked on all of us, but on the Jew more than any of us.

I think it was mostly Karushansky's own fault. For instance: After evening study time, we would come back, all ten sections of our year, one behind the other, marching in neat formation, one-two hup-hup, it could be heard all over the school. To reach our barracks we had to go past the Fifth Year's. And the Cows were there night after night, in the shadows, behind the walls, lying low. It was real scary. They looked more like starved wolves than Cows.

And who did they pick on? : Us, Section Ten. We were the smallest. We brought up the rear of the battalion and were scared shitless. When the other sections had made it safely past, they poured it on us. From a ways off, not coming too close, very quietly, making sure the lieutenant on duty couldn't hear them, Pssst, come here, Dog! they ordered us to fall out of the line. Come here, Dog! Quick! And we were so naïve, so stupid, we obeyed.

Well, only at first, because later, when we got to know that formation was something sacred, not on your life! With the lieutenant there at the head of the battalion, we were safe. The Cows would call us, getting furious, when we wouldn't even turn to look at them. They could go fuck themselves.

But not the Jew, he was different. As soon as he heard them calling him, Pssst! he'd fall out like a little lamb. And an hour or so later, when he'd already made at least twenty bunks, he'd show up in the barracks cool as they come.

In the beginning, we used to ride him a lot about it. Stupid, why can't you do like us? But he didn't give a damn, he shrugged, and walked away. As time went on, it got to be a simple routine and we got tired of teasing him, we were just wasting spit.

Besides—and you may not believe this—he even seemed to like it, no?

No. I believe you're going a bit too far. In fact, that year, in Third, they picked on all of us; we were Dogs, after all.

Yeah, but they were really hard on poor Karushansky. For instance: Several Fifth Year cadets would pop into our barracks. Somebody would call us to attention on the double. 'Tenshun! And we snapped to, eyes front, head straight, palms flat against our thighs, they knocked the shit out of us if we moved a hair. Slaps, a punch in the chest, right-angle position.

The thing is they got Karushansky every time, they could smell him miles off.

No kidding. They'd say, Name! And the Jew, who always went by the book—Cadet Karushansky Ávila Marcos! Then the Fifth Year man would roll his eyes, carry-you-what? And we'd give him the horselaugh. Quiet, damn it! Do I look like a clown, or what! the man from Fifth would shout. And we might be ready to bust a gut laughing but had to keep a straight face, or else they poured it on us too.

What's your last name? the guy would ask again. And the Jew, big as you please—Karushansky, sir! And how do you eat that? with a shovel? making fun of him. That's a Jewish name, sir! A Jew, huh? Yes, sir! So what are you? Jewish, sir! What? Aren't you Peruvian? Yes, sir, I'm Peruvian too! So why the fuck did you say Jewish the first time, if you're Peruvian? And he'd ram a fist into his chest, pow! 'Tenshun, damn it! Come on, chest out! Higher! Pow! he got it again. Jewish or Peruvian? Pow! Say Peruvian, damn it! Pow! Pow! Pow! Five, six punches in a row.

And it's hard to believe but Karushansky never let out a moan, as if his chest was made of steel. As hard to break down as an Indian.

But he wised up. Later on nothing could make him say he was a Jew. Jewish? Nossir! Peruvian. The trouble was, they had his number by then. Listen, don't try to play dumb with me, hey! What? Do I look like an ass? Nossir! Aha, so you're a traitor to your race, huh? Jewish faggot! Chest out, damn you! Pow! Another punch. The poor bastard really got it...

Sometimes they made him hop up and down the barracks, from the door all the way to the back wall, over and over again, holding a rifle up over his head and singing, remember?

Yeah. The waltz "My Peru" but with improvised lyrics... what were they?

They went something like "I'm proud to be Jewish and happy, so happy to've been born in the land of Israel," and more of the same.

On the other hand the professors and most of the officers liked him, didn't they? No, he wasn't an ass-kisser, or a drudge. But maybe the profs were impressed because he was a Jew. For instance, the biology prof, who always came into class half-crocked, badly dressed, shirt hanging out of his pants, remember him? we used to laugh our heads off.

He sure liked the Jew. You'll be a famous doctor some day, he'd say to him in front of the whole class. And we'd go over to him afterward and give him a bad time. Please, Dr. Karushansky, I'd like an appointment. I've got something real hard between my legs. Oooh! feel it, Doctor. He used to blow his top, his face got red as a tomato, but he never opened his mouth. He'd just turn around and go off steaming.

One thing we have to admit, he had brains, especially when it came to math. Prof would give us a problem, let's see, who has the right answer? Karushansky would make a dash for the blackboard, grab a piece of chalk, and scrawl numbers all over the place, like a machine, and in no time at all he had it. He always came up with the right answer.

The trouble was he was hard to live with afterward. Did we know who Einstein was? Just the number-one mathematician in the world, and a Jew too, put that in your pipe and smoke it! It used to bug us. All the great brains of history had been Jews. And not only in the sciences and literature but also in war. Didn't we know, really, that Napoleon . . . ? With a last name like Bonaparte? A Sephardic Jew! Columbus, Cortés, Pizarro, San Martín, Bolívar . . . They had all been Sephardic Jews, according to Karushansky. And of course we shouldn't forget Jesus Christ . . .

That's all we needed to make us want to get back at him. Some nights, when we were on guard duty, we'd sneak up to his bed and plaff! plaff! we'd slap him awake. Then we'd hide. He'd just call us motherfuckers, roll over, and go right back to sleep. No, we weren't trying to be mean, we were only getting even for all the crap he used to tell us.

Right: like the time he told us he'd been born in Israel and they had brought him to Peru as a young boy. That's why, he said, he could speak Hebrew. One day, he even started to teach us the alphabet, some really strange-looking signs. We were sure he had made it up and was trying to string us along.

Anyway, later on he admitted he was Peruvian and started telling us about his hometown—a whole bunch of weird stories, remember?

The weirdest was the one about one of his aunts and the mirrors. Listen to this. Any mirror she touched would immediately shatter into a thousand pieces. And that was only the beginning, because as time went on, all she had to do was look at mirrors and they'd explode. Sure enough the news ran through the whole town like gunpowder and nobody would let her into their homes. All she had to do was go out, somebody spotted her, and right away everybody'd start closing shop—the barber, the mirror man, the glass dealer...

No, he never did explain how long the spell lasted. All he said was they wouldn't keep any mirrors in his house for years.

Well, that story is a joke compared to the one about the earthquake. According to him, half the town was buried under the rubble... The ground swallowed them up.

Yeah, it caved in on top of them. And you'd have shit in your pants when you heard the rest of it. One day, a few years later, when everybody had forgotten all about it, all those people who'd been buried showed up in town, big as life. The end of the story? We don't know, because the Jew never finished any of his stories, not even once.

And that's not the only kind of stuff he bugged us with. For instance, the priest in Religion class talked about the life of Jesus and His miracles, and after class the Jew would always start in: So Jesus Christ is God for you, huh? He'd make fun of us. Aren't you kinda big to believe that crap...

And we all jumped him. What about His miracles? So? wasn't the Old Testament full of miracles? Didn't the Prophets perform thousands of miracles? What about the Resurrection? C'mon, how do you explain it? Nothing to it, Karushansky said. Before hanging Him on the cross they had drugged Jesus so's He'd look like He was dead. And then the apostles took Him out of His tomb and hid Him, on and on like that.

It used to make us mad as hell, and we'd lay into him. Sure, you Jews argue that He didn't die on the cross so's not to take the blame for killing God. The Jew blew his top. It's the Romans who crucified Jesus Christ! See? The Romans! And he walked away mad as hell. No, after a while we stopped listening, we knew all his damn stories by heart.

Was he a good soccer player? Who? The Jew? Hell no! In fact, you'd hardly call him an athlete. Not like us, we were always in the stadium working out or playing ball...

Yeah. Karushansky wasn't much good at sports. Or at maneuvers either. Yes, we had them on Saturdays, before getting out of school, in a big open field behind the school, about five blocks away. There were hills, imitation mountain passes, a couple of wild cane thickets, stretches of swampy ground, and the most awful stink everywhere.

We'd set out at the crack of dawn, with all our gear: rifle, helmet, and a pack. When we got to the field, our year split in half. One group was the attack, and the other the defense. Let's say we had to take a hill. We'd launch our attack, remember? howling like wild Indians, yelling, Hit the ground! crawling uphill, our bodies caked with dust. Charge! We climbed to the top of the hill and saved the day. But the Jew always straggled. He always had something wrong with him. I've got a cramp, I lost my bayonet, I turned my ankle, things like that.

So it's kind of strange he decided to go to Israel and join the Army. And even stranger, that he shot himself. Why? After all, Karushansky didn't like guns. He was terrified of them, I'd even say they made him sick to his stomach, right?

Look: Sometimes, once, maybe twice a month, they took us out for target practice. To a range over in La Perla, near the school. We were each handed six bullets and assigned a target: We'd lie flat on the ground and fire, pow! pow! pow! A few minutes later, the lieutenant would come by and we'd show him our shells to prove we'd fired at the target: Nobody had problems. Nobody, except the Jew.

Our very first time out, at his first shot, the rifle almost kicked his shoulder out of place. He never fired again. We made a bargain with him: he would give us his bullets and we'd shoot at his target. Then we'd slip him the empty cartridges real fast, before the lieutenant had a chance to catch us. That's why we really find it hard to believe he blew his brains out.

FIVE

: Thirty minutes gone and Peru is losing 2 to 0, and our star, Marquitos, is still on the bench, his eyes going right through the lush curves of Sandra, who is out of range : And Dr. Berkowitz enters our booth again to talk about the game :

"It's not a bit unusual for boys in boarding school to masturbate :
Some use a hole in a shoe :
Others the neck of a bottle :
Or even a pillow :
Some use spit : Vaseline : strong jets of warm water" :

Profound words from the most distinguished doctor, who cannot understand why, with whose leave, Lieutenant Montenegro is taking Cadets Karushansky and Aranzani to the school infirmary :

There simply is no way to stop Pelé : The Black Pearl has the ball : He swivels his hips trickily : dribbles past one rival and streaks like black lightning into Peruvian territory : Guillermo Delgado fouls him and the infraction is immediately called by Lieutenant Montenegro : better known as Iron Ass : ladies and gentlemen, he will not let this game slip through his fingers and he will not let Leoncio Prado Military Academy be overrun by fairies :

Watch him stride into the infirmary with determined step (one-two hup-hup) : tall, big-boned, wearing dark glasses, a pistol in his belt, he plants himself before Marcos's bunk : He pulls out a ballpoint : a notebook :

"Name and Section" :

"Cadet Karushansky Ávila, Marcos : Third Year : Section Ten," Marcos says, wishing the ground would swallow him : A cold, sticky sweat starts at the back of his neck and crawls down his spine :

"Who worked you over—what year were they in?" :

"I don't know, lieutenant" :

"What? Didn't you see their stripes?" :

"No, sir : They had on capes" :

"What about their insignia?" :

"No, sir : They weren't wearing caps" :

"Then how the hell are we going to know who beat you up?" :

Iron Ass's voice, folks, booms into every corner of the room : Marquitos flinches, as if they'd struck him across the back with a horsewhip :

"What's the matter? : Did I frighten you?"

Iron Ass looks at him and curls his lips into a sneer :

"Is that all you can remember?" :

"Yes, lieutenant" :

"Don't you remember how you got to the infirmary?" :

"No, sir" :

"Damn it! : I brought you here myself : last night : Do you or don't you remember?" :

But no, fans, Marquitos can't remember : And now, hands on hips, Montenegro eyes him : What's he waiting for? For Marquitos to thank him? : The boy does, to be on the safe side : Taken aback, Iron Ass throws him a scornful look that says what the fuck is wrong with this jackass :

"Thanks? You never thank anyone in the Army, or is that new to you?" :

He shakes his index finger at him to warn him against such dangerous play :

"Don't ever forget it, cadet : never thank anybody in the Army!" :

Montenegro drops his hand quickly, slaps his cartridge belt, and blows his whistle : Foul in favor of Brazil :

Vavá kicks it : a soft push-pass to Pelé : who takes the ball with his right foot, sets it up for his left, and his first-touch shot smashes into a goalpost and caroms off to one side : Excruciating moments of danger for Cadets Karushansky and Aranzani now on their way to the infirmary of this school that has given our country some of its most outstanding citizens : our country, forced this afternoon to play without our one and only Marquitos : Karushansky : Ávila :

Can Marquitos, who is sitting on the bench, possibly be thinking of his dear mother? : his gutsy Peruvian mother? : who stands her ground before the enemy team's center forward and takes a cannon ball in the pit of her stomach : DRINK INKA KOLA, THE PERUVIAN DRINK OF TOP QUALITY :

It will be such a comedown for Lima's Jewish community if he's expelled from Leoncio Prado Military Academy! : Should this happen, his father will never let him defend Israel's colors in the world soccer championship in Chile : Good, then he'll be able to play for Peru : Yes, he will be expelled for treason : for selling out this great country that took him into its heart :

Fans : Everyone knows old Karushansky's story : When he came from Bessarabia to Peru, he didn't have a pot to piss in : Yes friends : he set foot in Lima in October : on a drizzly day : during the procession for Our Lord of the Miracles through the streets of the city of viceroys : wave after wave of hooded heads : sputtering candlewicks : incense clouds : Christ (purple? black? mulatto?) on a litter : That day of days arrives and miracle of miracles : First, he's a peddler : brilliant at feints and tricky money deals : next step, opening a small store in town : then he meets Peruvian woman : And here, friends, we have the product of this holy union : Marquitos Karushansky Ávila! : Lima's biggest asshole reamer! : whose oversexed cock has soiled the honor of his family and his race : And all because he drove it into Cadet Aranzani's hole : and will not wear this afternoon the glorious red and white :

"If war was to break out between Peru and Israel : who would you fight for?" the guys from León Pinelo in the South stands ask him suddenly :

"For Israel!" Marquitos answers, not a shred of doubt in his voice:

"And suppose there's a war between Israel and Peru?" the Leoncio Prado cadets in the North stands now ask :

"For Peru!" Marquitos again without thinking twice :

Right on the ball! : because the kid's not an asshole, is he? : Peru in possession now, Tito Drago has the ball : he's the veteran inside right substituting for Marquitos in this contest : The old warhorse advances downfield with heavy step : like a caterpillar dragging its weight : Didí moves in to cover him : he takes the sphere away : he whips the ball over to the right where Bandy Legs Garrincha takes it : He breaks away up the sideline : Soria comes out to cut him off and fouls him :

Free kick for Brazil : Garrincha is still down, crumpled up in pain : moments of suspense for Manon, who tells herself : "I'd like to get pregnant and be a loving mother to my children" : Just like Marquitos's mother : a one-hundred-percent Peruvian who has turned him over to the center forward, a foreigner : and a Jew no less : It's a crime! : Where did he drive it in? : On the counter? : On his feet behind the door? : On the floor? : We don't know and wouldn't care to make a guess :

"Your mama's gone," Don Yehuda shoots at him pointblank : there's no trace of pain, suffering, or sadness in his voice :

Marquitos stares at him, eyes pleading for him to go on : But Don Yehuda has fired the foul shot and Marquitos squeezes his eyes tight, making believe he's asleep : And prays silently (the way his grandmother showed him : crucifix in his right hand : rosary beads in his left), he prays to Our Lady of Guadalupe as hard as he can : because, fans, ah! the kind and loving Virgin always protects her children, and Marquitos makes the sign of the cross under the covers, where Don Yehuda can't see, and prays to her to please let it be only a dream so he can wake up, at the first glimmer of daylight, to see mama entering the room :

And sure enough, his mother returns one day : crossing jungles, deserts, to see her son : her pregnant figure enters the room and once more Marquitos pretends he's asleep : lying on his stomach he thinks she's come to see if I've changed : she thinks I've been castrated and comes to see if I'm fat as a pig : He's opening his eyes : his mother is too heavy : she's five months gone : this time she carries a true Peruvian son in her womb : Marquitos climbs out of bed : He offers his mother the ring he has bought her : She accepts it : Marquitos strokes her face : then her shoulders : her arms : he holds her waist and pushes her gently, slowly toward the bed : But his mother rocks him with a hard slap! and the referee quickly calls the foul :

"Your mama's gone," Don Yehuda repeats :

Sitting on the bench in pain, his blood flowing

through him like fire, Marquitos won't let himself cry : not one tear comes into his eyes :

"Let the dead bury the dead," Don Yehuda says :

Pitaq wañurun? : His mother? : No : Marquitos knows his mother has found a place to stay at his grandparents' house : She's gone and won't come back : a fine example she's set for all the mothers of Peru : Off there in her hometown (baroque church, narrow medieval streets), the poor woman doesn't even suspect that her son's body is festering : a serious injury he got in the last game : tightly contested bout with blond Manon in the whorehouse on Mexico Boulevard : Marquitos looks awfully pale : his prick is rotting away : and there's very little chance he'll be out on the playing field on this sunny afternoon : SOL DE ICA : THE PISCO THAT GIVES YOU A LIFT AND CHEERS YOUR HEART :

Don Yehuda and Marquitos are forming the wall : there goes the free kick! it clips the goalpost and is deflected out of bounds : goalie's ball for Peru, now losing by a score of 2 to 0 after thirty-five minutes into the first half :

Seminario spurts up along the left sideline : he taps the ball to Vides Mosquera with his heel : Back to Seminario : who crosses the ball toward the Brazilian penalty zone : Gilmar comes out to pick the ball out of the air : and flips it to Didí who coaxes the ball, perfectly at home with it : And home is where Marquitos goes after school : He slips into papa's room quickly : he taps the ball and bends over to give it a kiss : The old man holds up the action : and tells him, you stand there front of me, so he can admire the uniform again : The old man's mind is on the magnificent Polish Hussars : the stands are restless : he hears cannons thunder on this afternoon when Peru doesn't stand a snowball's chance in hell without Marquitos in there :

The referee orders him, come say hello to your father : Show me how is marching in school : to the wall and about turn! by Garrincha who skips out of his marker's way : Marquitos's father backpedals to the danger zone : asking him, touch-and-go, if they feed him well in school : Marquitos takes the ball, thinking, What if they expel me : The old man's really going to miss the uniform! : His father takes off his pajama top : stripes and colors like in a concentration camp : He lies down on his stomach : Brazil is doing well in midsection : He asks him to give him a rubdown with camphor liniment : Marquitos caresses Manon's lily-white body : Brazil moving the ball well, at first touch : Didí constantly spurring on the guys in center field : a long lob from Didí to Zagalo : Brazil's forwards are switching places constantly : a killer pass centered into the penalty area : Pelé makes a diving header and the ball ends up in the net :

Goal number three for Brazil at the end of forty official minutes of play in the first half : This can't go on! : Folks, Peru needs Marquitos right now : It's high time he came out onto the field : LET US ONE AND ALL CALL FOR MARQUITOS TO COME ON OUT : Let the Republican Guards' band play the strains of our national anthem : And let us all sing together :

Koolod valeiva :
peeniima :
nefesh yehudi :
omiia :

Marquitos, one-hundred-percent son of Peru, must come into the game : He has a sacred duty and will perform it until he's given all he's got : who cares if they throw him out of Leoncio Prado? : ALL PERU FANS DRINK INKA KOLA : THE NATIONAL BRAND KOLA : We miss Marquitos this afternoon, and how! :

But still, there's the question : How well can Marquitos perform with the injury in his shooting leg? : DON'T SAY BEER : SAY CRISTAL : THE CHAMPION OF BEERS :

With the ball still floating over the midfield area, after Benítez's last-ditch return, the referee blows his whistle to end the first half : Marquitos leaves the bench and enters blond Manon's dressing room, and the question still is Will he or won't he play in the second half : We must insist, Marquitos does not go into the room of his Jewish friends' favorite whore but into that of Manon, whore of whores : Please remain in your seats, folks, we'll be right back with the second half of this game of games after the next commercial :

SECOND HALF

The next day was Sunday. His father went to the market to do his shopping and came back at noon, an Assyrian merchant stooping along, his shoulders heavy with sling bags bursting at the seams with all kinds of meat, fish, cheese, fruit, and vegetables. He put the week's provisions away in the refrigerator but not until he had sniffed at the meat, the cheeses, and the fish, polished the fruit with a piece of flannel, and sprinkled cold water over the greens.

Later, when he brought in the boy's lunch, his father announced the coming of the "three wise kings" like a town crier making his news public in a crowded noisy square. Half an hour later, he returned for the tray and was back the third time a few minutes after that. He started to pace about the room without saying a word, smiling furtively, as if he had a secret and was waiting for the right opening to let the cat out of the bag. Finally, he stopped in front of Marquitos, put on a serious face, and said: "I want you do me a favor; tell me story three wise kings, okay?" It wasn't the first time he made this request. And so, before starting the story, Marquitos always reminded himself to leave room for his father to fill in certain passages with his own dramatic, sly overtones.

This time, when Marcos finished telling the story, his father let himself fall back on the bed with a deep plopf! He was muttering gold, frankincense, and myrrh, surrendering to the lulling effect of those words, letting himself slide down the dark cliffside of the sheets, saying under his breath gold, frankincense, and myrrh, slipping out to sea on the wave of his song. His eyes had softened to match the gentle halting echo of his voice and his eyelids followed its rhythm, fluttering as if stirred by a summer breeze. And the son was repeating the same song in his mind, imitating his father's solemn rhythm and thus sealing at last the pact he would never break.

When his father announced the coming of the wise kings, with an exaggerated flourish in his voice, Marcos was in the bathroom. Barefoot on the cold, sweating tiles, he pressed on the rounded surface of his diaphragm to let the urine flow out more easily: he felt it swirl around in his belly, lash out like a coiled asp, release an electric shock through him, and come down at last with the lightning charge of a cloudburst. He let himself float in the fiery pain, spread throughout his urinary tract. It felt like a nest of wasps stirred up by intruders. He stood there, staring at the pool of bubbly urine and waiting for the sandstorm in his phallus to pass. Then he pulled the chain and watched his piss disappear, eddying down the toilet drain.

When he got back to his room his father's friends were there in a tight circle, whispering like nervous pigeons. The sweet-sounding modulation of Yiddish was like the cooing of voluptuous turtledoves and a proud puffing out of the chest and a sensual ruffling of feathers accompanied their words. At times like this, his father was a total stranger to him; in the harmony of gestures and words he seemed to recover, unconsciously, a lost wholeness, a more human countenance. On the other hand, his face would go through a sudden change as soon as he fell back upon the Spanish language: each phrase became a struggle to untangle a skein; then, he would look stern, clear his throat, jab the air stiffly with his hands, and look undecided, unable to get a foothold on the swaying scaffolding of words. Cold and cautious when speaking Spanish, the switch over to Yiddish raised the curtain on a scene stripped of all mumbling and fumbling. He was an actor playing himself; he moved about on the stage comfortably, not having to use histrionics, doing his part with strict fidelity, words and gestures in perfect accord. On his father's lips, the Germanic hardness of Yiddish became as soft as dough, it took on the many-colored refraction of the Slavic accent and dissolved into gusting winds that hovered on the edge of the

Bessarabian steppes. His discovery, when he was eleven, of this sonorous universe of his father's had awakened in Marcos a nostalgia, a nagging itch, a strange longing for landscapes he had never seen and vowels he had never heard: his father's whole story—all he knew about it were dates and the names of places scattered all over the world—opened in him a void he would have to fill later on with the vivid colors of his imagination. Through his mind would pass, time after time, the same sequence of remote images: long jaunts on horseback across plains punished by the sun's wide-open yawning mouth; he saw his father slipping around ambushes, going on to meet the night and never stopping to rest till he came to a noisy gypsy camp under a thick-leaved dome of trees in a forest. Then he dismounted and, all wrapped in the dim colors of his poncho, took his place beyond reach of the campfire's flames, gently stirred by a soft wind. Old gypsies, whose skin glowed, formed a circle around the fire, indifferent to the whirling sparks, flickering on and off like fireflies. The crackle of dry branches blended in with the jingling of tambourines marking the beat for a frenzied dance. The bodies of dancing youths and maidens were fused with the metallic, nervous excitement of the night, and their swaying movement seemed to follow the erratic flight of the sparks: a forge kept alive in the night by the erotic bellows of sensuality; in it those bodies took on the texture of melted, flowing metals. And then his mother would break away from the ring of dancers, move in between the firelight and the eclipsed figure of his father, and shed her clothes like a provocative Salome, flinging them into the air, inviting danger. Carefree and gay, she would then sidle up to his father, sitting cross-legged like an idol, and he would throw open the wings of his poncho and swoop her into them roughly, like a magnificent condor. The fire writhed sensuously and reached out to devour the soft contours of the night. Stung by the lapping flames, naked bodies rose like an ivy plant, roots locking together around the climbing spiral of the flames, until the sap's flow was exhausted and the plant's arms stopped growing. Leaves and stem collapsed to the ground, as limp as wax. Later, the couple said goodbye on a shore: his father sailed into the wind in a brigantine doggedly fighting off the pounding waves. On the sand, his mother lifted an arm in farewell, while the ship, climbing the waves far out to sea, showed her the fading blur of its stern with utter indifference.

The sound like scorched leaves Marcos's body made when he got into bed broke up the unobtrusive circle. The men stretched, lazily splitting up their huddle, and turned their eyes in the boy's direction. They were like three petty kings, fallen from their high estate, whom fate had thrown together in exile, secretive and full of far-fetched schemes for the recovery of their kingdoms. Their faces were as deeply lined as leaves and the small men made a perfect triptych of medieval rabbis who had wandered away from their ghetto. That's how Marcos knew them, always together in a perfect trinity.

The dark frown on his face made it clear that

his father was impatient to begin the ceremony. Holding up a glass of syrupy white wine, he took his place on the left side of the bed, to indicate that the show was now on. Leibel Gunn, the gnome with the huge cock, a veteran shopkeeper on Valladolid Street, who people said was living with a well-stacked black woman from La Victoria, stepped, gummy-eyed, out of the damp hothouse of his cave. He puckered his dormouse's snout in a funny way, took a package from his pocket and shyly put it into Marcos's outstretched hand. Then the gnome went back into the depths of his cave, where twelve grinning little mulattos waited for him. Marcos didn't know who had started the story, but it was common talk in the Jewish community, as well as an endless source of stories about sex for him and his friends at León Pinelo. Among the boys Marcos's age, Leibel Gunn had become a fabulous character, the high priest of rites still wrapped in mystery and celebrated only on the altar of erotic dreams or during the solemn rite of masturbation. In his nighttime fantasies Marcos had conferred on Gunn the title of supreme pimp who kept a large number of black women settled at strategic points toward the end of Mexico Avenue, a world his imagination had filled with mythological sea deities who twined their scaly bodies into a single giant knot. According to Marcos, the only way to explain how Gunn, the comic little dwarf-god, had become the adored lord and master of Lima's black women was the astonishing span of his cock. Marquitos had already opened the package Gunn had handed him and was holding his first gift: a gold-

plated Mogen David with which his father's friend ritually accepted him into the fold of the people of the Covenant. But in the boy's hands the six-pointed star seemed to have changed from a Jewish emblem into a glittering amulet given to him by a tutelary god of fertility.

"Let's see if you like this watch," Samuelito Rajman said in a subdued voice, bowing twice, almost like a count who has come down in the world and almost like a venerable rabbi yielding himself to the cadence of prayer. He didn't know how to use the familiar form of you in Spanish, although he spoke it well, with only a slight Polish accent and, forever hovering on his lips, the smile of a Jew grateful to live in this great country. Samuelito had a watch dealer's shop on Camaná Street, third block, and the customers were always right, yes indeed! no matter how far behind they were with their bills. The Three-Star Longines wrist watch he gave Marcos didn't need winding; always correct and trustworthy, like the best of his Swiss timepieces, Samuelito had seen to that. Marcos knew little about Samuelito Rajman, except that he had no family, almost no friends, and very poor circulation of the blood; this forced him to make room quickly for Don Jacobo Rapaport and go sit down tick-tock, so fine-mannered, tick-tock, on the other bed. Owner of YOUR FRIENDLY BAZAAR, located in the Mercado Central's labyrinth of trench-like passageways and superbly stocked with a wide assortment of clothing for cholos, Don Jacobo Rapaport thrust his toad's face forward, made his way over to the boy's bed with short hopping steps, *and laid a package on the feather quilt. It was beautifully wrapped in shiny paper covered with tiny stars and prancing little musk deer. Marquitos's eyes fell on the title of the book Don Jacobo had brought him:* A Small Jewish Boy Came out of the Ghetto. *"So you may read it before going back to school," he told him, using the tricky subjunctive as ably as he could, trying to speak like his aristocratic wife; she came from an old distinguished family and had given him quite a brood of light-skinned Peruvians, including blonds as handsome as their mother who had lots of blue blood running in her veins but no money. And since they were not at all wealthy, they lived in the Barrios Altos quarter but in an immense manorial home with large balconies all around it, in the viceregal style of a Lima* if I remain loving and dutiful it's only that you're still so beautiful.

When they had given him all the presents, his father offered Marcos a glass of wine to celebrate the special occasion; the old men picked up their glasses and regrouped around the boy's bed. Old Karushansky raised his glass, his friends did the same, and he made a toast: because today the people of Israel take into their fold a new member, it is never too late when providence comes knocking at your door, the old man was talkative and very happy, and next year comes Bar Mitzvah, he didn't have to grope for words anymore, he was full of ceremony, I am going give grrreat big party at home and will come all families and friends from new synagogue on Brazil Avenue. As kvater, *or godfather, Leibel Gunn asked if he might say a word or two, he made a big show of clearing his throat and addressed Marquitos "no shame it is to have bris now, because Ishmael have not had bris till was thirteen years old," and Samuelito, looking for all the world like a rabbi, said that the son of Moses had also been circumcised late by Zipporah, the patriarch's wife, who took a piece of flint, cut off her son's foreskin and cast it at Moses' feet, saying: Surely, a bridegroom of blood art thou to me. So it vass! So it vass! the three old men chimed in together, as if they had been called on to verify that the miracle was authentic, and then Samuelito, very poor circulation of the blood, went to sit over on the other bed where he started rubbing his ankles. Something between pride and amazement was in his father's eyes when he exclaimed, Yid at last! Yid at last! He had told his son, from the very beginning, not to say Jew, Jew is for them, for Peruvians, but Yid among ourselves. Did he feel like Yid now? More Yid or less Yid than before? Just as Yid? His father went on chattering in Spanish, his words coming out easily, thanks to the wine, Peruvian government should give us lands like to Japanese in jungle, so we can have new exodus and we all go to work land, no more shops then, we shut down all business and we go start kibbutz, we go put ourselfs to agriculture and also breeding animals, and the old man felt himself transported not only to fields tilled with loving care but also to bucolic scenes in the Bible. Each of the three old men assented in his own way: Samuelito was now rubbing faster, his blood was beginning to circulate again, color flowed back into his cheeks; Don Jacobo Rapaport seemed to be rising up off his feet, he gesticulated, groping for words without much success, a series of images he had seen the night before in the movie crowding his mind; Leibel Gunn had shrunk even more, he was listening absent-mindedly, sadly, and seemed to have sunk into the deep recess of some vague memory; but Marquitos wasn't listening to his father's words anymore: he imagined him in tunic and sandals entering the National Palace with a staff in his hand, going on to the audience room, right up to the president of Peru, I come only to ask for land nobody is working and if you say no, may a thousand plagues rain down on Lima! He had to cover his mouth with his hands to keep from laughing out loud, too sorry for his father or too scared to laugh at the old man's ideas, his weird tastes, like waking up and immediately turning on the radio to listen to the "Sol de los Andes" program, on which they played only* yaravis *and* huaynos, *some in Spanish, others was it in Quechua? And the old man, with his deep bass, would get carried away by the "If I could only be a hummingbird and you a pretty flower, I'd suck the honey from the bud of your red red lips . . ." Of course, he couldn't understand the songs in Quechua and perhaps because he couldn't figure out the words, he would lapse into a kind of trance, a stream of nostalgia welling up in his eyes. He was always saying, It's incredible how Yiddish and Quechua sound so much alike, the music also sounded so much alike because lalalala oh how sad, lalalala all my sorrow, lalalala all this bitter-*

ness, lalalala for this love . . . And he wouldn't stop humming the tune till he left for work. He didn't like Peruvian waltzes (he loved marineras, *because he was a great fan of the Alianza Lima soccer team, whose black players had the magic of jugglers with the ball), he hated everything Creole except the food. "Creole is two-faced," he would say heatedly. "Creole wouldn't hurt a fly to your face and all the time is trying to shove his finger up your* tochis *from behind." Or: "Creole doesn't like working either, lots beer, lots going out on the town but working, no deal!" or "Peruvian Creole is like Andalusian: woman, guitar, and bottle."*

According to the old man, Peruvian waltzes were music for wastrels, switchblade artists, and whores, nothing decent could be expected from people who spent their lives in bars and cheap underground joints, dens of iniquity all of them, where it was always the same, Be a good guy buddy and buy me anudder drink, I wanta get shhhtewed to the gills 'cause I'm feelin' sooo low, looook here my friend, I'm sooosad and lonely, a two-timin' woman made me suffer sooo; then the old man would make fun of all the cheap sentiment, all the unrequited love with its I've suffered all I can, I'm tired of waiting, days are eterniteees, stop torturing the man who gave you all his love, pleeeeese be compassionate; he would almost split his gut laughing at all that poor taste like there's no love without you, life's a bitter pill and there's no hope for me, come to me baby or I will die for you, die for you, die for yoooo . . . he simpered and mimicked, shake it babee, that's groovee, brother, here's to our Creole music, thrown in by the musicians between the lyrics, when they stopped singing and tackled the guitar with feeling, putting into it everything they had. But when it came to food, old Karushansky was a true Creole, although Dr. Berkowitz had warned him to go easy on fatty or spicy food because of his high blood pressure. From Monday through Saturday he stayed on a strict diet, chicken soup with vermicelli, boiled meat, and salad. But on Sundays he threw caution to the winds and gobbled down enormous quantities of food at each meal. He started with a very early breakfast at the Mercado Central in a small coffee shop owned by a Japanese who was a wizard at making crisp pork rind, and the old man would put away two or three rolls with sizzling-hot rinds and two or three cups of steaming coffee. Then he went shopping for the week. He was more particular about Sunday's menu than he was about the food for the other days of the week, when he had to watch his pressure. And the menu for Sunday's lunch was almost always the same: bluefish seviche laced with so much chili pepper it made his eyes water; Peruvian stew made with meat or shrimp or fish, also hotly spiced; and finally, baby goat or duck with rice and beans and, on the side, a Creole sauce with onions, lots of lemon juice, and ground cayenne. He never omitted the bottle of good red or white Tacama wine, whichever the menu called for, to slake his thirst. He always had fruit for dessert: green Italian grapes, watermelon or honeydew that, the old man suggested or even insisted, should be eaten with bread, the European way, because it tasted better and, anyway, fruit alone, just like that, was kind of immoral, an extravagance. After lunch the old man would go off to his room for the siesta and wasn't seen again till roughly six o'clock, when he emerged in bathrobe and slippers, hair all mussed up, lunging toward the bathroom. Then he would reappear, freshened up and younger, went through the living room, humming one of his favorite tunes, back into the bedroom, and made sure the door was shut tight. Around seven o'clock, he would come out again, impeccably dressed, and leave the house to go visit his brother Aaron who lived on San Isidro with his wife and three children, two very lovely girls—the younger one played the piano—and a terribly homely boy, who was flap-eared and skinny. At the corner, just down the block from his brother's house, there was an Italian candy store, open on Sundays, where old Karushansky stuffed his pockets with chocolate bars, chewing gum, and other candy to give to his little nieces and his nephew, who loved him so much because Oh, we have such a wonderful uncle! And he, First let's have a kiss and a great big hug. Before supper, little Rebecca would sit at the piano and the sweet, nervous, cute little thing would play "Over the Waves," the melody her uncle, who always brought her such delicious candy, liked best. Green with envy, Raquel the older girl, tried to win her uncle over with hugs and kisses. Skinnier and more flap-eared each day, poor little Simon, curled up in mama's arms, was out of the picture; she ran her fingers through his hair sheyner yingele, *my cute baby,* sheyner yingele *avoiding her husband's eyes, all that sissy stuff turned his stomach. For Karushansky the high point of these Sunday visits was dinner, which his sister-in-law always prepared without stinting on effort or money. They would all take their seats very correctly around a beautifully laid table. There was a red flower in a tiny bud vase filled with water, at each setting; a snow-white tablecloth and exquisitely embroidered napkins; glittering genuine silverware, and a seven-branched candelabrum for a centerpiece, as if the Pesach's Seder were celebrated every Sunday in that house. Old Karushansky felt happy at these* family *dinners, although he didn't get along with his brother, was he maybe envious? No, these were not his own children, but he enjoyed being with his nieces and his nephew, they understood everything said in Yiddish and had very nice manners. His sister-in-law was an excellent mother and hostess, a woman with lots of class, the perfect combination of the matron, a little on the old-fashioned side, and the modern, enterprising woman. In fact, she had gotten her husband to open a lady's shoe store for her in the heart of Lima's shopping district. She was a superior cook and served the best Yiddish meals in Lima, especially on Sundays, when all his favorite dishes filed past old Karushansky's grateful, nostalgic eyes: gefilte fish with hrein and sliced carrots, borscht with sour cream, delicious latkes with applesauce and finally, roasted chicken with kasha varnishkes. After dinner they talked about business or family matters, they were very worried this year about the elections that were just around the corner, and Aaron always harping on the same old tune, all Jews should vote for Prado, because Lord knows what Belaúnde has up his sleeve... And his sister-in-law wanting him to tell her everything about Marquitos, how is he doing in school? Is he still having trouble with Hebrew? Don't worry, he'll soon catch up with the rest of his class. Does he still get headaches? Maybe it's his sinuses, don't you think a visit to the doctor would be a good idea? And old Karushansky, yes, she was perfectly right, everything his sister-in-law said was good, such an intelligent woman she was... He would have loved to remain forever in his brother's house, but once the conversation ran out, he knew it was time to go, and so he would say goodbye till next Sunday with a strong handshake for his brother, kisses for the children, who were in bed by now, a light peck on his sister-in-law's perfumed white cheek, and then he would head for the street reluctantly, with a look that said,* Sunday after Sunday, I visit your home, when will next Sunday be comin' around *cielito lindo* to drop in again? *He always got home very late. His father, Marquitos thought, probably went to see his friends, Gunn probably took him to a whorehouse and, like a good fellow Jew, loaned him one of his black women: a real tall one with fleshy lips and big sexy hips. In the whorehouse his father got laid, or did he? And Samuelito? And what about Don Jacobo Rapaport? He could easily imagine Gunn astraddle the wild jet-black mare, after all, didn't he have a well-earned reputation as a high-class pimp? He found it a lot harder to imagine his father and the other old men on top of a black woman, the old buzzards probably couldn't even get it up anymore. They most likely got together on Sundays to have a few drinks, play pinochle, and just talk about the happy days of their childhood long ago, far away in countries whose musical names cast such a spell on him.*

But the sweet cooing of the turtledoves had struck up again: a faint buzz of voices was filling the bedroom, and there sitting around a small table heaped with food, were the four old men swaying naturally to the music of their conversation. To Marquitos, Yiddish seemed to perform a series of varied stunts, in the mouths of the old men: ich ken nicht *was a cartwheel,* du geveizn *a flying leap,* iz geshtorbn *a somersault, and the easy flow of the cadence took on the elasticity of a contortionist. Seeing them there, completely carried away by the full effect of the wine, noisily pecking at the grapes and the olives, stuffing themselves on soda crackers and sardines, sealing the Covenant with their little feast around his father's table, Marquitos felt that he was trapped in the middle of a ritual as interminable as one of those biblical voyages in which you had to wander for forty days and forty nights without rest. But where did the voyage begin, where did it end? In Dr. Berkowitz's office? Seven days later, when they took the stitches out? At this moment, second day of the crossing, Marcos sensed that the rite still had a long way to go, it left the confines of the room, went beyond a simple phimosis operation, branched off into two trails wandering like streams over rocky beds, sank into the ground to unravel a maze of passageways, continued through vaulted caverns that might be a church or a synagogue, and finally came to a crossroads, where father and son became one? Relaxed by the chorus of the old men, Marquitos started to fall asleep. Their figures began to blur, as if seen through a soap bubble, and to evaporate, leaving a kaleidoscopic play of colors behind his eyes. Before dropping off, he saw his father's silhouette about to sit at his side to watch over his sleep and he had the imposing appearance of an Abraham squatting at the gates of hell to prevent those who bore the sign of the Covenant from falling in.*

ONE

: Well, fans : here we are, back again at José Díaz Stadium with the broadcast of this sensational game that will decide who'll be the South American Soccer Champion of 1962 :

And don't forget : Brazil only needs a tie to become the tournament's undisputed champion : Consequently, Peru will have to come back onto the field and go for broke : And if need be, ready tc draw blood : like the great Samson on the walls of Saksaywaman drawing blood from the Philistines in the days of Marquitos's forebears:

But this means Marquitos has to rejoin his team : Marquitos Karushansky Ávila : All our sports fans are with you at this painful time and won't let them kick you out of school : All the hopes of the Community rest on your shoulders : a Community badly in need of another Jewish soldier in its ranks, like in the old days : Yes siree, folks : like Field Marshal Rodrigo Ordóñez, a Sephardic Jew : one of the outstanding leaders in the conquest of Peru! : After all, who here doesn't remember his great exploits? : He was in more battles than Pizarro and Almagro put together : He fought all the way from Colombia to Chile : far, far to the south : As a young man, he was one of the four who captured Francis I at Pavia : and he also played a big part in the sack of Rome : He finally died fighting against Pizarro in Salinas de Cuzco : And in spite of all his great deeds, his name lies unjustly buried in oblivion which, we all know, is the second shroud of the dead : Fans : ON TO VICTORY ONE AND ALL! : AND DRINK SOL DE ICA! :

The players of the two teams are now returning to the field : Play will get under way again in just a few seconds and we'll know then if Marquitos is in his usual inside right forward position : Red-and-white jersey number 8 :

The players are now taking their places on the field : A colorful formation for Lt. Anibal Montenegro to report to the Colonel, director of Leoncio Prado Military Academy :

> "At fourteen hours on Wednesday November twenty-second of the current year : the undersigned : Lt. Anibal Montenegro Marino :
> Surprised Cadets Marcos Karushansky Ávila and Javier Aranzani Ampuero :
> Fifth Year :
> Section Ten :
> hiding behind a locker in the aforesaid section's barracks : Therefore : in full knowledge of acad-

emy regulations : the undersigned who detected something strange in the air : led said cadets to the school's infirmary : where they went through a medical checkup :

According to Dr. Belisario Márquez, on duty at the time, this examination revealed that :

Cadets Aranzani and Karushansky were guilty of wrongful behavior that was beyond doubt morally damaging to the good name of Leoncio Prado Academy" :

These very serious accusations are made just as the referee blows the whistle to start the second half of the match : And sure enough, ladies and gentlemen, we see now that Marquitos has come in to replace Tito Drago : Bedlam! : Kusi! : The place has gone wild! : A standing ovation in the whole stadium! :

"Whip 'em in the front : chahuee! :
And whip 'em in the rear : chahuaa! :
Chahuee! : Chahuaa! :
Marquitos! : Marquitos! :
Rah! : Rah! : Rooh! :
Long live Peru!" :

And long live Marquitos Karushansky Ávila! : A true-blooded Peruvian! : born on the same day and month the Spaniards, four hundred years ago, captured the last Inca : Atahualpa : And here's Pizarro now, surrounding the stadium with his army : Atahualpa appears on a litter and with him his faithful entourage of fine nobles : Father Valverde goes up to him now and hands him the Bible : in a dangerous play! : and says to him : "This is the word of God" : Atahualpa holds the book up to his ear : he frowns : "I don't hear anything," he says and hurls the Bible through the air, away from him : What gall! : folks : So now the Spanish team starts firing, giving no quarter : Hundreds of Indians fall on the field and the last Inca is taken captive : and yet the referee, Adonai Elocheinu, does not call foul play : Mana nii atina on the referee for not calling it! : But tukuy imapas manam wiñaypaqchu kausan, tukuymi tuquyniyok! : How true : Nothing lives forever, all things come to an end : says the Talmud . . . :

But, ladies and gentlemen, we haven't come to the end of this game yet : and Peru has the ball : Terry feeds it to Marquitos : who quickly passes to Vides : he feints : and loses one opponent : he feeds it back to Marquitos : Seminario breaks away up the left side : and Marquitos is moving up to the eighteen-yard mark : The whole red-and-white forward line is deep in enemy territory : Ball for Seminario : He sprints toward the left-corner flag and centers the ball toward Brazil's goalmouth : Marquitos traps the ball with his chest : he drives a fierce, well-aimed grounder and the ball slams into the left post! : and falls back into the penalty area : several players scramble for the ball : and Zózimo is just able to clear it into midfield :

Peru has come to life! : That was the first time Gilmar really has been in trouble : DRINK INKA KOLA : THE REFRESHMENT WITH THE REAL PERUVIAN TASTE : And now for all you parents : Here's an announcement of vital importance : Do you want to lift the spirits of your children and gladden their hearts? : SEND THEM TO BETAR HAFLAGAH! : With us here at our mikes is the man who leads Betar Club : Zev

Jabotinsky! : Let's listen to what he has to say about Betar :

"One thing is clear to me :

Betar is not a political party :

It is not a school :

Not an army :

And yet it takes in all three of these :

But there is more to it :

A special spirit we all look up to as the ideal of every man, every Jew, every growing person :

In sum : Judaism, youth, humanity" :

Yes folks : Garrincha in possession : He passes quickly to Pelé : The score is 3 to 0 in Brazil's favor : Marquitos faces the Black Pearl : a man-to-man battle of soccer Titans, and Marquitos gets the ball! : now he's advancing up the Leoncio Prado parade grounds: Switching the action to the right side of the field : Joya streaks after the ball : Peru is on the march : A backkick from Joya to Alberto Terry : who returns the ball to Marquitos in midfield : He goes past the main building with Cadet Aranzani and Lt. Anibal Montenegro : Brazil's defenders in tight formation : Marquitos heads the ball beautifully over to Vides Mosquera : who shoots a first-touch ground-level shot straight at Gilmar's body :

Gilmar kicks the ball into midfield : It soars over to the infirmary : Marquitos's father is nowhere in sight : He hasn't come onto the playing field to be with his son who is in pain : when our country's honor is at stake : He must have shut himself up in his room, a high mound of underbrush covered with cobwebs and dust :

"Your father is scared stiff of empty rooms," Marquitos's mother says, holding her head in her hands :

And it may just be true : because the house is such a tangled nest of furniture and junk, there's no room to breathe in it : It's like a jungle : The only light in it comes through the patio door and all the walls are full of pictures : print after colorful print of a place Don Yehuda calls Israel : It's so far away, across the sea, you need a plane or a ship to get there : And he also says, with a very solemn face :

"There I am going some day : I don't know when : Kausayka mayu jinam reaching down to the sea, and I not going let myself die in this country, nosir" :

He says it like that : in the funny way he has of talking : And when he goes it will be on a ship : because when he was young he dreamed of being a sailor and he would give all the gold in the world to be eighteen, maybe twenty, again and ship out to see the world :

That's what he said the day Marquitos and his mother arrived in Lima : Watch them on your home screens : Mother and son loaded down with bundles : Don Yehuda is there too : He's about to see his son for the first time and wonders if he has done the right thing, bringing him here : In the West stands his friends leap to their feet to tell him, at the last minute, he had better leave the boy in his hometown : But Don Yehuda can't go back on his word now : He has certain obligations and can't leave his son to shift for himself : Still, the thought of having to live under one roof with Mercedes, Marquitos's mother, doesn't appeal to him : and Doña Mercedes wants to know what's in it for her : she's in Lima only because of her son : he has been driving her out of her mind insisting that she should take him to meet his father : So finally, against her better judgment, Doña Mercedes says okay and one fine morning they make the trip : It's Marquitos's first trip ever : But Mercedes has been there : only once, when Don Yehuda sent for her : and she came back saying : The gringo wants me to take him his son : Yes folks : the gringo : it's what the family calls him : the gringo! : because grandpa says Don Yehuda is not a Peruvian but from some country far away where they talk a very peculiar language : And you should have seen how happy old grandpa was when Mercedes came back from Lima with the news :

"So what are you waiting for?" he told the boy : "For the gringo to come and get you?"

And grandma too :

"If I were in your shoes, I'd start packing : because the gringo, being as he's so nice and such a gentleman, will give you everything :
Haven't you always dreamed about this?" :

But she's really passing him the ball : sarcastic : piercing her husband with needle-sharp eyes : and most likely thinking about what she's always told her children :

"In my whole life, I've never seen such a tightwad as that shitty old bastard!"

Fans : it's true : Because with the pennies the old man doles out to her, the poor woman has to work miracles to make sure there's a few crumbs to eat in the house : where grandpa slips in and out like a shadow : exactly like Marquitos's father who is nowhere to be seen on the playing field : And is being paged urgently over the stadium's loudspeakers :

"Señor Yehuda Karushansky : Go to the school infirmary right away!" :

A few more yards and Marquitos will make it to the infirmary : He's in the penalty area now : he taps the ball to Wild Man Seminario : who floats a butterfly centering pass toward the goalmouth : Marquitos lunges : a diving header! : Gilmar stretches for it like a cat and : Goooooal! : Gooooooal! : Gooooooal by Marquitos! : Gooooooal for Peru! : A killer pass by Seminario and a fantastic play by Marquitos exactly five minutes after the start of the second half : the score is now 3 to 1 :

The notes of a *marinera* now flow into the stadium to spur on Peru's team : People in the stands stamp their feet : White handkerchiefs spring to life and flutter in the wind like doves in flight : The entire stands at the León Pinelo School are beautifully festooned today as we celebrate Independence Day : Yom Ha-atsma-ut! : A day of glorious sunlight and wild excitement : Thousands of people mill around in the patios and hallways eating tiny skewers of shish kebab : Schoolboys and schoolgirls rush out onto the playing field all at once to dance a *tondero,* a *marinera,* or a popular waltz : Because we Peruvians are like that : cheerful : happy-go-lucky : like our country full of striking contrasts : islands of vegetation in the middle of a sea of sand : impenetrable valleys : snows and mountains : We're all that and much more : says the director of León Pinelo in his patriotic speech

"Neither pure Spaniard nor pure Indian :
We love one another standing by the flag and at the foot of the altar :
We love one another in the temple, the shelter that makes us feel as safe as in our own homes:
that picks up our first cries when we are baptized :
blesses us on our happy wedding day :
and receives us after death like a loving, caring mother" :

That's how it is : On with the show! and DRINK SOL DE ICA : THE PISCO OF OUR INCA FOREBEARS! :

Brazil advances up the left side : Zagalo carries the ball : He gets all tangled up with the sphere and then it slips away from him, rolling out wide, and the referee signals goalie's ball for Peru : Seminario receives : He passes to Vides Mosquera on the opposite side of midfield : Vides lets sail a long boot... and Gilmar snaps up the ball easily : Midfield again : Pelé tries to thread his way through two defenders but they take the ball away from him : Peru on the march once more : Terry : Over to the right side of the field again : his pass to Joya is much too long : Didí gets it for Brazil : He looks for Garrincha over on his right : There goes Bandy Legs : Soria clears well toward Calderón who now starts going up the field with the ball : He backkicks to Marquitos : The school's doctor is on the lookout : Man-to-man marking on the turf : Lieutenant Montenegro never takes his eyes off Marquitos who has the ball : a deep pass to Cadet Aranzani : The doctor and the lieutenant block his way : They order him, a real cutie with his Sandra Dee babyface, to kneel down : chest pressed against the side of the bed : The doctor gets ready to come onto the field : He's warming up : First, a vigorous rubdown on Cadet Aranzani's abdomen : He runs into a hard lump in the area : Coming fast around his right, Dr. Márquez parts the boy's cheeks from behind : A cold sweat rolls down Sandra's face : Dilation of the anal cavity : The doctor makes a deep pass : Marquitos tries to get away through the right side where Lieutenant Montenegro is marking him : If he can get past the school's iron gate, they'll never catch him : But Marquitos stays put, rooted there : Break away through the left side!, the crowd lets out a frantic roar! : Don't stand there like an idiot! : Cut across the field fast! : Our country counts on you! : Run! : Quick! : But maytam? : where to? : that's the question burning in every Peruvian heart : And, ladies and gentlemen, there's only one clear-cut answer, and it's sacred : To Israel! : On a ship, because it's so far away : Come on, Marquitos : hurry! : The ship is about to leave : Leaning over the side of the pier, your father is saying goodbye : his blue-and-white handkerchief flutters like the graceful wings of a dove : A foul, the referee calls without thinking twice! He will not let Marquitos leave this land of his birth before the final whistle of this game : And remember : DON'T SAY ADONAI : SAY WIRACOCHA! :

TWO

He broke the news that summer, shortly after we got back from camp. The Leoncio Prado? Are you crazy? Impossible. Cut out the bullshit. Who was he trying to kid? We were a little too big to swallow that. But Cholo insisted, he wasn't trying to kid anybody. He was serious. In fact, he'd been preparing for the entrance exam for two weeks. And us, what a bullshit artist! Where? And him, in a preparatory school—every morning, Monday through Saturday. And he stayed home afternoons boning up.

He said the exam was very tough. There were thousands of applicants from all over the country each year: from the coast, the Andes, and the Amazon jungle. So he had to work his ass off studying. And us, brother, how stupid can you get. What a way to waste the summer. It was a lot more fun spending the day at the beach. Or playing soccer at the Hebraica. But Cholo said no. He was sick and tired of the León Pinelo, and he didn't mind giving up things as long as he got out of there.

The León Pinelo School? No sir, by then it was already one of the best schools in Lima. This was after it moved from Jesús María to Orrantia Street. Really a beautiful place. It had cost a fortune but was very modern and had everything. Fully equipped classrooms, spacious, with lots of light coming in all the time. It even had a soccer field.

And wow! It was regulation size. Yessir, we didn't have to play jampacked together like before in the old school. Now we could spread out all over the place and yell our heads off.

That's right. We didn't have to run scared that they'd knock our blocks off. What's more, this time they put a great big blue wooden star over the gate. We didn't have to hide from people anymore. These were modern times. We had started a new wide-open, easier-going life.

Still and all, Cholo wanted out. All he told us was he couldn't stand the place anymore. But why? Who knows? Hard to say, but he must've had a reason, no? What about his studies? Look, I'd say he was a bit on the lazy side. He was getting lousy grades. He almost flunked in freshman year, you guys remember?

Yeah, that year he barely squeezed through. He had to catch up on a couple of subjects that summer. I seem to remember they flunked him in math.

He kinda didn't have a good head for numbers, see. Prof used to call him to the blackboard, give him a problem, and Cholo, poor guy, would start squirming like he had ants in his pants, couldn't make heads or tails of the stuff. He'd begin scribbling the first thing that popped into his head—then he'd sit down shame-faced, looking like he wished the ground would swallow him.

But nobody could stand up to him in Jewish History. Top of the class, knew it backward and forward. And come to think of it, it was really strange because there, where they didn't even give us a grade, the guy worked his ass off studying...

And strangely enough it was the same in Pre-military Training. It was a stupid course. Our instructor was a chunky first sergeant, remember? Kind of Indian-like, with a huge potbelly, he looked like a big clown.

The dumbhead acted like we were in the Army. He used to swear at us and order us around like soldiers, but we'd put him in his place right off. Hey sir, just a minute! How about some respect, you're not talking to a bunch of Indians! The poor shit used to turn red as a beet. He'd beg us to excuse him. Please don't get me wrong, he'd say, staring down at his toes, he was so used to Army life, i m sorry, boys, I know I get carried away sometimes.

And since he couldn't do a thing to us, he boiled over inside. But Cholo Marcos took all his crap seriously. Obeyed all his orders, studied very hard and, naturally, got the highest grades. Look at the way he carries himself! the sergeant would say. Learn from Karushansky! Cholo was well on his way to being named the number-one monitor in Fifth Year, at the 28th of July parade.

But all the other subjects seemed to slide off his brain like water down a duck's back. He used to start all kinds of trouble in the halls and they were always sending him to the principal's office. And some days he had to stay after school till five o'clock, all by himself. No, it never did him a bit of good. He'd put on a brave act and tell us he couldn't care less if they punished him. Cholo was a real oddball. He did some very strange things. One day he brought a rubber into class, remember?

Right. We were in Hebrew class with *moré* Zusman (our nickname for him was Rosita). The *moré* turns to write some crap on the blackboard, Cholo takes out his condom, blows it up, ties a knot around its mouth, gets up bold as they come, and lays it on Rosita's desk. You should have seen his face when he saw the balloon on top of his papers! He started to squirm, he was red as a beet, speechless. Then we all burst out laughing but Cholo, very deadpan, raised his hand and without batting an eyelid, said, *Moré,* I found this little balloon on the floor. Rosita could have cut him to shreds with his eyes. And then he finally found his tongue again. Scoundrel! Wiseguy! Filthy swine! Where had he learned such things! He hustled him out of the room, pulling and pushing him, and screaming This is the last straw! This time we're really going to expel you!

No, he wasn't kicked out of school. Cholo played it straight. No, sir, the condom wasn't his, he'd found it on the floor. The guy had some balls! A real sharpie. There wasn't one girl in class he hadn't given a bad time. He pestered them right and left. He'd sneak up to them quiet as a cat and zowie! grab their ass, squeeze their tits. Or else he would steal up from behind and start pumping...

No, Cholo wasn't the only one who did those things. He had a sidekick, a guy named Linzer, we called him the Maniac. He aped everything Cholo did—he was a real ventriloquist's dummy—followed him around like a puppy. He was half crazy and had a slight stutter. Whenever the recess bell rang, he'd make a beeline for the toilet to jack off. One time, we caught him red-handed and we started to tease him, Prick-puller, what are you hiding there? You're gonna go blind jackin' off all the time. And him with his runny little bat's eyes, No, nothing, I was only taking a leak. Cholo was there and took up for him, he was his buddy, go on, lay off him, damn it! And you know what Linzer did? Something that turned our stomachs—he got down on his knees and kissed his hand, remember? Marcos stared at him, disgusted, with eyes that said, We may be friends but not that much... Wow!

No, Cholo pestered the hell outa the gals but they never complained. They just stood there gawking at him or asked, Hey, where'd he come from? What's wrong with him? But something strange happened one day. We were in Religion class. Professor Cuevas suddenly appeared at the door, walked in, and whispered something in the rabbi's ear, like this, and then made signs to madman Linzer and Marcos to follow him. There was nothing strange about him taking Linzer out of the classroom,

Cuevas was the school's psychologist. But we couldn't see where Cholo came into it.

We found out later, when we asked him, What happened? Why'd they pull you out of class? They had taken them, him and Linzer, to the Psychopedagogic Department. And then? Nothing, Cuevas had given them a kind of test: a lot of very strange questions—word games, riddles, numbers, geometric figures, mixed-up sentences they had to unscramble. Well, was it tough? And him, Shit no! Easy as playing ball, a real joke. What about Linzer? Linzer had complained the whole time, the questions were too hard, he was getting a headache, and what not.

Then us, Did he know why they had given him the test? And Cholo, No he didn't, but he couldn't care less, what he wanted to know was why the fuck were we asking him so many damn questions. And us, Aw nothing, don't get sore, brother. But he stared at us like he didn't trust us, like he was trying to guess what the hell are these guys thinking, right?

And what we were thinking was they gave him the test to see if he was crazy. After all, we shouldn't forget he was always trying to molest the girls.

Exactly. And one of them must have squealed, for sure.

Personally I think it was Fanny. She was terrified of Cholo—the son-of-a-bitch used to sneak up from behind and zowie! his hand would reach up under her skirt. And poor Fanny would spin around completely freaked out, eyes popping out of her head, ready to start crying.

Sure—we always used to talk to him about it. Brother, you've got to cut it out. It's no way to treat women. But Cholo, what do you all know about it, we were babies, morons, faggots.

Yeah, we were in Second Year when they gave him the test, and you know? maybe it's why he decided to switch schools. But why the Leoncio Prado Academy? We couldn't get over it, because the stories we heard about the place were enough to make your hair stand on end.

Look—the Leoncio Prado was a kind of reformatory they tried to pass off as a normal school. Parents put their sons in there to have them straightened out because they couldn't do a thing with them. People used to say it was a place for degenerates and delinquents. What's more, he had to be sick in the head to want to become a boarder and live the life of a dogface, away from his family and his friends.

As a matter of fact, we couldn't figure it out. But he was dead set on it and when we saw this, we tried to change his mind. Don't be a schmuck, brother! Think it over! Use your head! What all didn't we tell him! remember?

First and most important: he wasn't going to find a single Jew there. The officers were ballbreakers, not a single day would go by without them knocking the shit out of him, and so on. Is that what he wanted? Still, Cholo wouldn't listen, always gave the same identical answer: we were a bunch of faggots.

No, when he entered Leoncio Prado he wasn't living over on Breña anymore. He and his old man moved into a boardinghouse downtown, on Huancavelica Street. I believe it was around the corner from Cailloma, wasn't it?

Yes, and it was run by a lady from the Community. All kinds of rumors about her went the rounds of our houses—that when she was young, right after coming to Peru, she had become a . . . how shall I put it . . . ?

The word you're fishing for is *whore*, isn't it?

That's a very hard word. After all, we're talking about Menachem's mother. Menachem? The best *madrich* Betar ever had. Before leaving for Israel, he had been *madrich* in our *kuvsa*. Yes, Marcos's too. We all belonged to the same group.

But let's get back to Doña Raquel, Menachem's mother. When we knew her, she already had the boardinghouse. She must have been about fifty but she was well preserved, wasn't she? She was a stunning blonde, her wavy hair falling all the way to her waist—full of fun, and a real gabber. She loved to laugh. She'd burst out laughing at the drop of a hat, and she had a way of doing it that was carefree, open, mischievous like a little girl's.

When Menachem went away to Israel, Doña Raquel stayed behind with her daughter, Shoshana. Next to her mother, Shoshana was the other face of the coin: a weirdo. Sometimes, on a Saturday afternoon, Menachem would invite us to his house and Shoshana stayed in her room the whole time, and if she did come out, she just hung back there, a little ways off, staring at us with those big nostalgic eyes of hers, like she wasn't really there . . .

And then she'd disappear, flapping her arms like a butterfly.

What a weirdo! Skinny, pale, kind of freckly. Shoshana must have been maybe three or four years older than us, at the most. So when Cholo moved into the boardinghouse, I figure she must have been about seventeen. She had already left the León Pinelo. They apparently took her out of school in her junior year, right? Must have been because she was so strange. One look at her and you could tell she had a few loose screws.

No, no—she wasn't the violent type. She was more of a melancholy type, well... more like a romantic heroine.

Yeah, mysterious. There was something very sad about her, no? Her old man? All we knew about him was that he was dead. But the strangest part is, nobody in the Community knew anything about him, not even his name. So naturally this made people invent a lot of things about him. One of them, that Shoshana (and Menachem's) father was Señor Karushansky. Mere rumors? Jewish community gossip? Who knows! We were not about to ask Cholo, so there was no way to find out...

Okay: the thing is, Cholo got himself into the Leoncio Prado and we stopped seeing him for quite a while. Almost two months without news about Marcos. Then one Saturday he dropped in, right out of the blue, at Betar. In uniform!, remember?

He looked like a chocolate vendor in a movie theater. Yes, it was his uniform, with all kinds of buttons and gold braid—a cheap, tacky imitation of the uniforms they wear in American military academies.

So Ackerman, the one who used to heckle him the most, pulled a coin out of his pocket and asked him to sell him a "Sublime" bar. He got the horselaugh from all of us and Cholo said, Okay cut the shit. But how could we, with him looking so damn funny! To make things a lot worse, they had shaved his head and he looked like a Prussian soldier. What's happened to you, brother? Did they get you when you were asleep? And Cholo serious as all get out, That's how they cut everybody's hair at school. How come? Were they all full of lice, hey? And Marcos, Cut it, that's enough of all your fucking shit.

And that's where we stopped teasing him, he was really a sad case. The poor guy had come in uniform to show off, most likely to impress the girls, but it had backfired. The others started to make fun of him the minute they spotted him. Hey, why the party outfit? We didn't know it was Carnival time! Where's the party gonna be? They kidded him so much, it was the first and last time we saw him in uniform.

Yes, we kept on seeing him at Betar on Saturdays after that, but Cholo kind of gradually drifted off, didn't he?

At first we hardly noticed but it became very obvious, after a while. You almost never come around, we'd say to him, but him, he had other things, he also had to see his Leoncio Prado buddies.

Sure, he told us a whole bunch of things about his school. They've got you by the balls, haven't they? No, we were all crazy. From the start, he refuted, point by point, everything we had told him about it before he went there. A real hell? You couldn't be more wrong. Just the other way around. The teachers were better than at León Pinelo. But didn't the officers horsewhip him? Heck no! Real A-one people, all of them. What about the guys in Fourth and Fifth, didn't they give him a bad time? No, things like that weren't allowed.

That's what it's like : Don't talk to me about León Pinelo! Which is the best school in Lima? Leoncio Prado, by far. There's no comparison, man. No? Let's see, what school marched with the Air Force, the Navy, and the Chorillos cadets in the 28th of July parade? Only one! Which one? Whaddya mean, which one? Leoncio Prado!

What a big showoff, and it was the same when he talked about maneuvers. Do you guys know how to shoot? No? Well, I do. And not just a rifle but also machine guns, mortars, bazookas. Besides, they were also teaching them how to parachute jump. We weren't sure if he was making it all up—anyway, we'd tell him to go tell it to his grandmother! Cholo would blow up then. You don't believe me, huh? Okay, no problem, any day now I'll take all of you to the school so's you can see for yourselves. When? Any day soon, what's the rush? Liar, he never did take us.

How could he, when it was all just lip? Like when he promised to bring the Leoncio Prado soccer team to play against León Pinelo. You'll see what good soccer really is, we'd better start getting in shape, we're going to swamp you under. And did he ever bring it? Hell no! It was just lip talk. When the time came around, Cholo argued that the Colonel wouldn't let them come—like we could actually swallow that crap, no?

No, he never introduced us to his Leoncio Prado friends. First it was, Do you all want to come to a fair at my school? Then, How'd you like to come to a party at the home of some of my buddies? But it was always pretty soon now, he always came up with the same lame excuses, I'm sorry, guys, I forgot to let you know, I fucked up, he swore over and over again he hadn't done it on purpose, I promise to, next time...

Who knows, maybe he was ashamed.

But what I'd like to know is, ashamed of his friends or of us? What d'you think?

His friends? They all came from good families and lived in Miraflores or San Isidro, so they weren't trash. Their fathers had money. On Saturdays when he didn't go to Betar, he went with them to country club or the Regatta Club. They swam in the pool, played soccer, he (Marcos) was introduced to the girls...

Next to the Regattas, Hebraica was nothing, he used to tell us. There were no broads at Hebraica. And he was always telling us about how great the Peruvian dolls were. They weren't like Jewish girls. Peruvians weren't so goody-goody—they put out, they liked a good time, remember him saying so?

And we'd lead him on. No kidding! C'mon, tell us some more. And then he'd get all wound up with his stories. Peruvian chicks? Hot, horny, real yummy. But did they or didn't they put out? At this point Cholo would stop talking and go like this, with an evil wink...

No, we didn't fall for any of it, heck no. But anyway, we told him we'd like to meet them, when are you gonna introduce us? And Cholo, any time we liked, any Saturday now I'll take all of you to the Regattas. Pure bullshit! He never did.

No, we hardly ever mixed with Peruvian guys. And even less, of course, with the chicks. Like, they all lived in another world—parallel to ours but with us almost never crossing over to their side. Hard to say why, it's only that they had their life and we had ours, a different one. Still, Cholo managed to go in and out, as he pleased, from one world to the other. He wasn't like us...

What about Jewish chicks? No more. After entering Leoncio Prado, he stopped bothering them. By then we all had steady girls, the whole bunch of us went out together—to the movies, to the Tambo, to the Cream Rica. Besides, we saw them everywhere all the time: at school, Betar, Hebraica. And you shoulda seen how terrified of him they were, wow! He had built up a bad reputation, they wouldn't have anything to do with him. For a while, he asked them, one by one, to be his steady, but none of them would have him. Then, to cover up, he'd say, Why would I want to go out with kids who still wet their beds. Let them learn to wipe their asses first. And he'd go back to the same old tune—It was a lot better to go out with Peruvian broads, they were more down to earth, not so full of tricks.

And another thing, he liked to play around with Indian girls, remember?

It was really something, enough to make you piss in your pants laughing. He'd come to our houses and head straight for the kitchen. Then he'd start acting like the dudes in cheap TV soap operas; he'd start trying to make out with the poor servant girl. What's your name, where you from? Did she have a boyfriend? And what did she do on her day off? And he'd tell us to get lost, not to be so damn nosy, you're gonna cramp my style. Then he'd kinda close the door and the son-of-a-bitch would feel them up.

Well, it's what he said afterward, and with all the rich details thrown in, step by step. First, he'd feel their tits—then he'd start working his hand in, very slowly so's not to get 'er scared, between her legs. And down with her drawers! I zip down my fly and then— Then what? we'd ask all excited. Then nothing, he'd say with indifference, and he'd pass his finger under our noses, smell, you jack-offs, and us with our tongues hanging out, drooling.

No, we didn't fool around with servant girls, though we sure would have liked to. Sometimes we were lucky to have young ones in our homes, rosy-cheeked like apples, nice. But just imagine what our parents would have said! Most likely they'd 've had a stroke. Plaff! They'd 've keeled over, on the spot, humiliated and ashamed. Isn't that right, guys?

Right! Like the time in my house, no? When my old lady caught Cholo in the act, kissing the girl. Yeah, they were in the kitchen, and Marcos was on top of the Indian girl, on the table, remember?

Jesus Christ! Your old lady was fit to be tied! She grabbed Cholo by the ears. Pig! Scoundrel! Zass! Zass! A couple of hard slaps. Savage! Wretch! Get out of my house!

Actually, he had it coming, because that was going too far, a bare-faced insult. We had warned him lots of times, Stop fucking around. One of these days you'll get caught. But him, same as ever, Who cares, what can happen to me if they catch me?

He was right. Nothing. Except that from then on he could never come around to your house again, right? Besides, it was his own funeral. Our old ladies must have passed the word around, because afterward when Cholo came to our homes, they would look at him with suspicion, thinking, Watch out for this boy, he's a bad influence...

Well, they weren't far off the mark either, because Marcos always acted older than the rest of us. I remember how he insisted on taking us to "Mexico," a big rambling whorehouse in the suburbs, a hick place, near La Parada, just outside of Lima. At first we told him he was crazy, we were still just kids. What if they won't let us go in? But Cholo, Anybody can go in there, don't be such fairies, let's go.

We went. But scared to death. At night, like in the movies. Lots of tough-looking characters, one after the other, filing in and out of passageways, like ants in an anthill. And inside, room after room, and through half-open doors a face peering out, half a body, a leg, women for everybody's tastes, in all colors and sizes: whites, Indians from the Andes, from the Amazon, in all varieties. They winked at us, come baby, come right in, I do the works, complete service. And us, pinch me, am I dreaming? But Cholo acting very experienced, Let's see now, which one do you guys like? No, not tonight, we were so damn nervous we didn't feel up to it.

We spent the time going up and down the passageways all night, just looking on. And all of a sudden, who d'you think we discovered there? Who else but Marcos's old man? No, we saw him a ways off, going into one of the rooms. Cholo stopped in his tracks, petrified, and we played dumb, and he said, Let's go, and of course we didn't know which way to turn, we followed him out.

No, we never went back to "Mexico" again with Cholo. In his shoes, we'd have done the same thing, no? Look, what if you ran into your old man, do you think you'd have gone back? Not on your life!

THREE

: Pelé takes the free kick : Over to Vavá : Who feeds it to Didí : Back to Pelé : He chips the ball and it grazes the crossbar on its way out : It's Peru's goalie's ball :

Guillermo Delgado, the Lion of José Díaz Stadium, will put the ball into play : Marquitos traps the high pass well : He's controlling the No. 5 well now : Pushed from behind, Marquitos rolls over the turf and the medic on duty calls the foul :

"Let's see, what have we got here?" Dr. Márquez says, blowing his whistle : He takes the chart off the bunk and glances over it quickly :

"Nothing serious : it's a very simple operation : First we'll remove the adhesive tape" :

Marcos clenches his fists, pushing down hard at the same time : Now he's reaching one hand up to his eyebrow :

"Stop scratching!" the doctor breaks in, putting his finger on the exact spot where the foul was committed : "What happened? Did you trip?" :

No response from Marcos : The doctor throws him a compassionate look : he applies some ointment : and puts a fresh tape on :

"Ready," he says, lifting his arm for the indirect free kick :

Marquitos himself will kick : Come oooon boys! Full steam ahead! : Go, go, go! : Let's do it for Peru! : Marcos drives a hard shot at the far corner of the goal defended by the school's Colonel : A fine header by Belini clears the ball : It drops out of bounds : Peru's throw-in : Marquitos takes the ball well : Lieutenant Montenegro moves in for the challenge: Peru's inside wing is in danger : He gets all tangled up with the ball and the lieutenant has no trouble taking it away from him : He makes a fake movement, looks over to the left side of the field for Marquitos's father who today, Saturday, is in his store, and orders him to come to the infirmary at once : Don Yehuda Karushansky can't make up his mind what to do : In the meantime, robbed of the ball by Iron Ass, Marquitos pries open his eyelids and his eyes meet a blurry film : it's the mosquito netting's gauze, fans! : But now he's staring at the doorway, half expecting his father to appear :

"I wonder where the old man is?" Marquitos asks himself :

And tormented by this heartbreaking question, he pictures his father in the middle of nowhere, laid out on his back, numb, covered with dust : Marcos is in a cold sweat : He shuts his eyes and his head swells up with screaming voices, erupting steadily from mouths that sway back and forth in all four stands: North, South : East, West : Thousands of mouths with elastic fleshy lips growing into one enormous reddish-purple wave that slowly curls and turns into a single jeer :

"Your father isn't here because he's watching the store," the stadium roars, taking on the arched shape of ugly lips frothing and breaking into peals of obscene laughter : Yes folks : soccer fever at its height here in the stadium! : All the stands rise in one long-drawn-out cheer, Peru! Peru! Peru! : And there on camera, Marquitos writhing in pain, while the rumble of voices starts up again : insinuating, drumming a long list of things into his head : all the things that come between him and his father in every part of the field :

"How many times I have to tell you to go around only with Jewish friends?" Don Yehuda says :

And it's true : the Peruvian team is favoring the right side of the field too much :

"You go straight home and I don't want see you talking to those hoodlums!" :

Peru's coach seems very worried :

"Or else one of these days I pack and go away for good and you never find me again" :

The Brazilian team is getting away with murder, playing dirty when they have the chance : the players are obviously letting their nerves take over : Folks, this is not a game for anyone with a weak heart : The ref, Reb Goldstein, who was certified in Jerusalem and is the maximum authority on the field, has a crucial decision to make : Is or is not Marquitos a Jew? : He cannot allow such intentional violence against our country's star inside wing :

This electrifying contest gets under way again : Vides Mosquera receives : Seminario breaks away into open territory : A back pass to Marquitos : Searching anxiously for his father, who never comes : Brazil recovers the ball : Didí has it at the twenty-minute mark of the second half : Turns it over to Vavá : who crosses a good lob and Pelé makes a flying leap into the air to head the ball : and just look at how calmly Montenegro snags the ball, what confidence! : Marquitos is wide awake : The referee is now checking his watch : The stadium clock marks five thousand years of Jewish history : Marquitos picks up a low pass : Watch that boy handle the ball! : He uses all the wisdom of his forebears to stop the ball. . . ! when peleh vafeleh, miracle of miracles, a shadow appears in the infirmary door : It's an off-side flagged by the linesman : On the free kick, Belini serves the ball to Don Yehuda : The old man comes in with his head down; he's dragging his feet under a weight of forty days and forty nights : He's going over to his son's bed : There's nothing in his way : The old man pulls a chair over and sits down : Centuries pass while he waits there : Defensive tactics by Marquitos, who draws the covers up to his chin : He turns away : Embarrassed silence between father and son : There's a faraway look in the old man's eyes : Marquitos is on the verge of stealing the ball away from him : He's about to ask him to hold his hand : to clear away the anxious feeling spreading in his chest : But Don Yehuda fidgets, shifts in his chair, crosses his legs and his arms like an imposing Abraham : The ball hangs in the air : Over the boundary line :

"Come Saturday, you start prepare for Bar Mitzvah," Don Yehuda says, trying to make the ball keep still :

Marquitos takes his words in, caught off-balance : Like the rest of us : Shame on him for not pausing to consider his son's injury! : his son, who has this painful rupture in his chest :

"How is possible such things happen in school? : They worse than animals! : Who did it? : Fourth or Fifth Year?" :

"Third," Marquitos parries, stealing the ball : His father follows close on his heels up to the half-moon area :

"Third Year? : Sure you not lying to me?" :

"No," the boy protests weakly :

"So why they beat you up?" :

"It was a fight : they were insulting me" :

"Insulting? : How?" :

"They called me a dirty Jew . . ." :

A superb direct shot by Marquitos, trying to surprise the goalkeeper! :

"Is nothing they call you dirty Jew," nimble as a cat, Don Yehuda stretches for the ball and snares it : "It don't matter they call you dirty Jew : And if same thing is happening again, don't fight : Play dumb and keep walking : You're only Yid in school and is better not looking for problems" :

Yes folks : Marquitos is fouled again and takes a hard spill, rolling over and over, as if down a sandy hill, humiliated and ashamed of himself : Because everybody knows, fans, that Jews can't stand the sight of blood! :

"But," in the West stands the Pinelo's principal leaps into the fray like a cat, "look at all the surgeons our school has produced over the years" :

And so every Saturday at this same time, Helene Curtis asks the sixty-four-thousand-dollar question in Peruvian currency : What does it mean to be Jewish and/or Peruvian : Answer this intriguing question and go on to the second round of our sensational contest :

Let's see : To be Jewish and/or Peruvian is :
Ser :
Estar :
A lucky star :
It's to be from a country of sharp contrasts :
It's to let the country go down the drain fast :
It's to have a Hebe Mame :
Or a screwed-up Mom :
It's to warn a Jewish Mother :
It's to belong to a race :
To pray for belongings :
To look for spiritual guidance :
Or be a misguided spirit :
It's a people :
Not a steeple :
A religion :
It's to populate a region :
A confluence of races :
A race against integration :
It's Zionism :
Cynicism :

Nonism :
It's crazy :
A destiny :
A necessity :
Something foolish :
History :
Hysteria :
What is it? :

Check with a cross or a star the answer you think is correct and go on to the next round of our friendly Helene Curtis contest, where every question is worth sixty-four thousand dollars in grushim gold : our show brought into your homes by your very own Channel 4, the station that is in perfect tune with the whole nation : Peru now in possession, Marquitos with the ball :

Marquitos tries to get around the question : Rabbi Goldstein and Father Camacho come out to challenge : A scuffle for the ball on the left side of the field : Each man on the Brazilian team is marking his own man : Marquitos misplays the ball, passing it to Don Yehuda : Who bungles the question and gives it right back to Marquitos : who easily dribbles past the rabbi, leaves Father Camacho sprawling on the grass, shoots with his left... and Don Yehuda has to punch the ball clear :

Once again Peru has the ball : Soria : Forward pass to Vides Mosquera : He breaks into the clear up along the right sideline : Peru is playing very well : Heel pass from Vides back to Terry : He backkicks it to Calderón : Joe Calderón lifts a long ball toward Marquitos : who goes into the penalty zone with two rivals on his heels : he crosses the boundary line of the River Jordan : and the Rimac : he sets up the ball for his right foot : Fires a hard grounder and . . . Goooooooal! : Goooooooal for Marquitos! : Karushansky : Ávila! : Goooooooal! : And Rabbi Goldstein just stood there flatfooted, like a statue! :

Second goal for Peru, ladies and gentlemen, after twenty-five minutes of play in the second half : The score 3 to 2 in favor of Brazil : USE KOLYNOS AND SMILE : The stands are a sea of waving flags! : Red and white? : Blue-and-white banners? : And just take a gander, friends, at the happy face on the president of Peru, His Excellency Don Manuel Prado, sitting to the right of the Colonel, director of Leoncio Prado Military Academy : celebrating with patriotic fervor our national team's second goal : Yes folks : Let us stand up and sing together :

"Let our banner soar and toss :
Higher than the Southern Cross :
Let its wake fill our sky :
With a trail of glorious light" :

And remember : DRINK INKA KOLA : THE PERUVIAN REFRESHMENT MANUFACTURED BY PERUVIAN HANDS IN ALL PARTS OF PERU : COAST : ANDES : AND AMAZON JUNGLE :

Well folks : With this sensational goal our Marquitos has just proved his unequaled love for this land, Daughter of the Sun, where the dauntless Inca chose to live : And if Peru marches on to victory this afternoon, he will surely not be kicked out of school : In a supreme act of sacrifice, Marquitos forgets all about his pain and goes onto the field to fight his heart out : This boy is the pride and glory of Peru : He has the brains of the Jew and the physical stamina of our native Inca : Yes siree : Head in Jerusalem and heart in Cuzco! : Our most heartfelt thanks to his devoted parents who gave our country a soccer player with their son's unique talents :

Brazil lines up for the kickoff : Doña Mercedes, Marquitos's mother, is the goalkeeper : Dr. Berkowitz, the left wing : Rabbi Goldstein playing inside right : Father Camacho in his usual position at center half : Dr. Márquez at fullback : Señor Yehuda Karushansky playing center forward : Referee : Lt. Anibal Montenegro :

The whistle blows and Pelé taps a back-heel pass to Zito : Opening to the right for Garrincha : He sprints up the right sideline like a streak, meets the ball, and crosses it to Vavá : But Guillermo Delgado is right there to clear the ball with his head : Peru recovers : Benítez with the ball now : Diagonal pass to Joya : Joya backward to Calderón : Fine precision passing by the Peruvian team : Marquitos receives : How beautifully he dribbles the ball! : Like he was dancing a *marinera* : There goes Belini charging in, aiming for his leg, but Marquitos sidesteps him with a quick hip movement : He's almost up to the eighteen-yard line : Nilton Santos is waiting there : Marquitos setting the game's pace : more stomping in the bleachers : more drumbeats in the stands : "God was born in Laredo and the Virgin Mary in Trujillo" goes the song : Nilton rushes him hard : Marquitos nutmegs him, passing the ball between his legs : Father Camacho comes out to block him : Tries to cut him off but Marquitos skips out of the way, dribbling the ball toward center field where he crashes into the rabbi who commits a foul as big as

Lake Titicaca and Marquitos falls flat on his face : This simply cannot be tolerated, folks! : The Brazilians are dealing out kicks, shoves, elbows right and left, and the referee just looks the other way! :

This is not soccer, it's more like a knock-down-and-drag-out match : And the playing field, a green boxing arena! : which Marquitos enters for the evening's main event : In one corner, arms leaning on the ropes, Iron Ass has his eyes on him, his lips pursed in a sneer : a few yards away from the mat, a sea of lead-colored heads rocks back and forth : A heavy sky floats over them like a wrinkled canopy : Three hooded figures step into the ring : an ear-splitting roar of applause greets them : They drop their hoods and Marquitos recognizes the three Fifth Year cadets : The lieutenant comes over and blows the signal for the fight to begin : The Fifth Year men fan out, trying to surround him : Marcos isn't the least bit intimidated : he smiles at them calmly : They attack him but he skips back out of their way : to one side : over their heads : The Fifth Year cadets bounce off the ropes : they snarl viciously: and they charge again with their fists up : They've got him backed into a corner now, but Marcos scrambles free between their legs. : The three swing at him again : huge curling horns seem to sprout from their heads : frustrated, they bellow : lower their necks and charge : But they miss their target : Ladies and gentlemen : Watch Marquitos bobbing and weaving in and out like a cat : constantly moving from side to side of the ring : End of round one and the others are already groggy! : Their legs get all tangled up : they stagger : they go down flat on their faces on the canvas : And there's the lieutenant blowing his whistle and separating the players to stop them from mixing it up on the playing field : FOR UGLY HEADACHES : BUFFERIN SPELLS RELIEF :

But Marquitos is still crumpled on the ground, badly hurt : And there is Iron Ass going over to tell him to get up, right-angle position and cut out the act : But no, folks : Marquitos is not putting on an act : his pain is real, pure, sacred, ecumenical : And if you want to see good acting don't miss the year's most exciting opening tonight : THE JEW : a play packed with drama, suspense, fun, laughter, and tears : Tickets on sale at the synagogue on Brazil Avenue : Single performance at 8:00 P.M. at the Colón Theater, located in the heart of downtown Lima : at the corner of Plaza San Martín and Huancavelica :

And there are Marcos and Don Yehuda comfortably settled in the first row of the balcony : obviously impatient for the show to begin : They are the only Lima Jews at the opening! : The lights dim out and the curtain goes up :

Act One : a small stoop-shouldered man with a nose like a corkscrew walks out onto the playing field, wearing a black overcoat that trails down to his ankles : he carries a suitcase tied with a string to hold it together : He asks for a room, right off the bat : The landlady leads him upstairs to the back of the boardinghouse : They trade a few trivial words : The last part of the first act is now on : and suddenly, in a shifty maneuver that's never cleared up and that the referee does not sanction, old hook nose takes over the boardinghouse : The former landlady is now his cleaning woman : A fantastic play applauded and cheered by the audience in all four stands, as the curtain drops! :

Act Two : The small man with the hooked beak, in a fine pin-striped suit and patent-leather shoes, in his new role as financial wizard is expertly answering several telephones at once : a heart-rending scene then follows in which a secondhand dealer's business and his family problems come into play : A daughter about to get married to a goy : A crooked son with the police on his tail : and a lot more like it : The act ends with the merchant throwing his arms up in a gesture of concern and defeat :

Act Three : Quite old now, white-haired and with a face creased with fine wrinkles, corkscrew nose lies dying in his sickbed : Surrounded by his family : The old man opens his eyelids a little and says in a voice from beyond the grave :

"Moishe, are you there?" :

"Yes, papa. I'm right here" :

"And you, Leo, where are you?" :

"Here, papa, next to you" :

"And you, Raquel, my dear daughter?" :

"I'm here too, daddy" :

"And you, my beloved wife?" :

"We are all here with you, Jacob" :

"Then damn it, who the hell is minding the store?" :

That's the first Jewish joke Marquitos heard in Lima! Like a bomb, the ball comes flying at him : And now, upset by the treacherous guffaws filling every tier in the stands, he doesn't know what to do next and serves the ball by mistake to the rabbi who, in a beautiful give-and-go with Father Camacho, sprints into Peruvian territory and makes our boy look like a monkey : The defense tightens up : The rabbi keeps dribbling upfield, driven by the natural doggedness that is so much a part of the Jewish character : He turns it over to Pelé : who gets past Guillermo Delgado and with his left foot blasts a rocketlike shot that smashes into the crossbar and flies over it : What a close call for Peru! : But folks, it's high time we put an end to the rising tide of catcalls and deafening laughter that fills the stadium : Because to try and make a sap of Marquitos now that our country's honor is at stake is clearly an unforgivable act of treason to the Fatherland : This is his homeland too and we'll see that he's buried in it! : Fans : Do you want to feel at home? : Visit our ZION REAL ESTATE INC. AND BECOME THE PROUD OWNER, at modest prices! on easy terms! of your own, your very own little acre in the HOLY LAND : AND LET'S PLAY BALL! :

FOUR

He told us he lived over on San Isidro, in Los Pinos, first block, but we never saw his house. No, not even from the outside. And yet almost all of us lived in that part of town, near the golf course or next to the club.

Some five blocks from where Karushansky said his house was. But no one around there knew him and we had never run into him in any of the places we went to, then.

So we had our doubts about it. He saw this and changed his tune. No, he said, I've just moved out of the neighborhood, before that I lived over on Jesús María, next to the Jockey Club, see?

Then why do you take a different bus when we get out of school? Because I go downtown to see my old man, the Jew said. According to him, his old man had a store, the biggest of its kind in Lima, where he sold only imported cloth, cashmere from Scotland, English flannels. Really? Where is it? And him, Right in the middle of Jirón de la Unión, at the corner of Ica. But as he was forever trying to impress us, we had our doubts about it.

And us, How come we never run into you in the neighborhood? And him, It was because he went to see his Jewish friends on Saturdays and Sundays. Ah, maybe that's why we've never seen you at the matinees at the Orrantia movie theater, we, throwing him a suspicious look.

He told us about a place where he met with his Jewish friends on Saturdays. Some kind of club where they prepared them to go to Israel. And on Sundays? On Sundays I go to the Hebraica, he said, a club for Jews only, recently built on the edge of town, an enormous place with a soccer field, a swimming pool, much bigger than the Country, the Regatta . . .

He said it like that, very proudly, overdoing it. Like when he talked to us about his famous León Pinelo, no? The best school in Lima! And of course we argued with him, defending our old schools. How about the Champagnat? C'mon, what d'you say about Roosevelt, Lincoln, La Salle? And the Jew, all those schools shrank up next to the León Pinelo. C'mon tell me, how many times had we won the Radiant Sun trophy for the best school in the 28th of July parade? : The León Pinelo? Three years running, in case we didn't know.

And also, how many languages did they teach

in our schools? In León Pinelo? Five: English, Hebrew, French, German, and Russian. Okay say something in Russian. And the Jew, easy as pie, I've been talking Russian with my old man ever since I was little. What, didn't you know my old man was Russian? And not only that, he could speak ten languages. And right there, he'd say a couple of crummy words that sounded more like Quechua than anything else, right?

And us, trying to get his goat, how do you say motherfucker in Hebrew? But the dope didn't catch on, he said it, puffing up, pleased with himself. We didn't know if he was putting us on. He had built up a reputation as a liar from the start and even when he'd swear up and down something he said was true, we wouldn't believe him.

Like the time they took him to the infirmary and the story went around that some guys from Fifth had pounded the shit out of him. When he came back to the barracks three days later, the poor guy was a mess, all patched up with adhesive tape, and with a swollen eyebrow. Of course we tried to make him feel at ease. Brother, those mudderfuckin' Cows really cut you up, sons-a-bitchin' bullies! And him, What's all this crap you're handing me? Who gave you that story?

And d'you know what he told us? He'd had a fist fight with two guys from Fifth. From Fifth? Where? In the latrine. How many did you say? Two. What year? From Fifth. Aw, go on! Yeah, we called him a liar, Go tell it to your grandmother. And the Jew, I don't care if you don't believe me. Well, how come you ended up in the infirmary? He said he couldn't remember, he had passed out, couldn't we see he had a split eyebrow?

A tall story, no? Where was he going to draw all the strength to square off with two guys from Fifth? Look, not even Vega, the husky Indian in our section, a big tough guy, a real thug, would have tried to go that far. Vega? A goddamn son-of-a-bitch, a hood who bullied everybody...

But he was harder on the Jew than on the rest of us.

You're right. He had it in for him. One afternoon, I remember, the Jew had a special pass and was putting on his uniform, when Vega, wham! pounced like a gorilla and, plaff! landed right in front of Karushansky's locker, hands on hips, spoiling for a fight. Then he told him, Are we gonna square off here or in the bathroom? The Jew froze and Vega leering at him, like this, like he could have swallowed him in one chunk, peering at him. By then the rest of us were taking it all in, There's gonna be a fight, let's go watch it. And Vega went on, Faggot Jew! Say something!

And Karushansky, meek as a lamb, I've got to go home now. We can fight tomorrow. Tomorrow? Vega said, moving like he was going to jump him. At this point, the Jew covered his face with his arms but instead of hitting him, Vega looked at us. Did you hear that? Faggot! And he faced the Jew again, Look, don't fuck with me. We're gonna fight right now! Karushansky turned white as a sheet. It's true, brother, not now, I can't. You could tell from his voice he was ready to shit in his pants. Then Vega shot him a dirty look. Faggot Jew! Look at the way he's shaking! Karushansky didn't move a muscle and Vega was still tearing him to pieces with his eyes, twisting his mouth. None of us budged. And finally the Jew said something. You don't understand, they called me from the hospital, my old man is dying. When he heard this, Vega squirmed: he squinted at him; he looked like an ape, forehead screwed up, scratching his head. Then he shrugged, spun around, and went to flop into his bunk. The Jew made the most of this to finish changing his clothes and flew out of the barracks without so much as throwing us a glance.

He returned the next day, looking down-in-the-mouth, something was wrong, you could tell from way off. Your old man? we asked. And him, Yes, he was still in the hospital, cancer of the stomach, he only had a few months left. From then on Vega laid off him, wouldn't even look at him. The Indian wasn't such a mean tough, after all.

No, we never heard anything more about his old man. None of us ever tried to touch the subject again. For us kids, a sick, dying father was nothing to laugh about. So no one ever found out if he died.

But we were talking to you about the fight Karushansky was supposed to've had with the cadets in Fifth. A change had come over the Jew. He became more of a street tough. Sure, they still kept going after him, same as with the rest of us, but he caught on, got smarter. Before, you'll remember, he would step out of ranks the minute he was called. Not any more, he played dumb, and kept going.

Yeah. He even started letting up on his studies, but he went on getting good grades. That year he was named Distinguished Cadet three times straight and even got to be head cadet of his section a couple of times, didn't he?

We used to give him a real bad time because how did he get all those good grades without studying? Ninety in Chemistry without cramming? How come? The chemistry teacher looked kind of fruity, so we'd ask him if he was fucking him up the ass. And the Jew staring us right in the eye, sure! Didn't we know it? He fucked him in the bathroom. When? During recess. Was it fun? Super! he'd say. D'you see now? He wouldn't let others beat up on him anymore, he wised up.

That's when we let him into our group. But actually, he had already been wedging his way in gradually. A bit timidly at first, but afterward real cocksure of himself. He latched on to us like a shadow anywhere we went; he treated us to cigarettes, to soft drinks at La Perlita.

Yes, we all knew one another before entering Leoncio Prado. We came from the same neighborhood, almost all of us had gone to the same school. So it was natural for us to form our own group. But it was different with Karushansky. He wasn't like us. He was out of place, really didn't fit in with us.

No, no, not all! Our gang was nothing like the "Inner Circle" in the novel you just mentioned, a book full of lies, things made up so as to run our school down. No sir: there were no street boys or degenerates among us. A bit wild, yes. Full of pranks? That too, but very different from the Jaguars and Boas who formed that famous "Inner Circle," see?

Exactly. Because we didn't steal copies of exams, or fuck chickens in the stadium, or go into La Perlita to jack off. No sir. Our school wasn't anything like that. It was a tough but well-disciplined life. We weren't saints but no one can accuse the school of being a hell.

Our group? It was formed right after we started Third. We always hung around together, we stood up for one another. The whole section envied us because we were all so close, like musketeers, no?

That's how it was. And nobody fooled around with us. Whenever anybody tried it, we ganged up on him. Even Vega stayed out of our way...

Well, maybe he wasn't scared. Let's say he respected us. Ah, those were great days... And not just in school but also out of it. On Saturdays we went from one party to the next, wild parties with nonstop dancing; we danced a lot of *merengues*, remember?

Sure, with Xavier Cugat and his band. I remember one year they came to Lima at Carnival time. They played for two nights at the Regatta. And with that eyeful, Abbe Lane, no less! What a broad! Not much of a voice, but what a pair of knockers!

And the way the damn woman danced! You can't imagine those hips: they were hot, she threw them around like she was on fire. Jesus man, what a great time we had at those dances! And not only *merengues:* we also played soft music, very slow, perfect for grinding. And then we'd dance with our girls like this, holding on to their waists, giving 'em the knee, our lips brushing each other's cheeks, we didn't give the poor gals a chance to get their second wind...

Karushansky? No, he didn't seem to be much interested in that kind of thing. We used to ask him but he never came to our parties. And afterward at school, nothing but excuses. I couldn't make it, brother, my old man was sick. Or else it so happened that the same Saturday as the party, some coincidence, right? he'd had to go to the synagogue, what lousy luck... And so on, one story after the other.

He showed up at only one of the gang's parties, you guys remember? And what did he do? Nothing—acted real shy.

Exactly. And did he make out?

No. And there were a helluva lot of girls...

And did he ask any of them to dance?

No, not even that.

And when the Jew left, what did the girls have to say?

What a bore, so dull!

And d'you know why? Because the Jew was out of place in our world, that's why. He wasn't like us. Do you remember the suit he wore to the party?

As old as Methuselah: it looked silly on him, he looked like a clown. He wore the same thing when we went to "Mexico" together. He always showed up looking like a real hick, right? with the kind of sweaters and shirts only an Indian would put on...

Yeah, he had weird tastes. It made us feel ashamed for him. We couldn't go around San Isidro wearing stuff like that...

We'd've had to be out of our minds. What would

the chicks have said? They'd probably have thrown rocks at us, right?

No, we all used to wear the same kind of clothes in school: low black boots, khaki uniform, and a heavy green cape, in winter. The dress uniform was different: indigo flannel trousers and jacket, three rows of gold buttons on the chest, gold epaulets too, embroidery and badges on the sleeves, and finally, white kepi. When kids from other schools passed us in the street, they yelled, Chocolate vendors! at us. But they were probably green with envy.

No, we can't say it wasn't a pretty tacky uniform.

But it was a real hit with the girls.

Yeah, right, but only with girls from the lower classes—because girls from Miraflores and San Isidro just laughed at us. So we took off the uniform the minute we got home.

Sure, we laugh at it too now, but at first we could hardly wait for them to give us the damn uniform, remember?

Well, our enthusiasm didn't last very long—and later on we were ashamed to go out in uniform.

And imagine! some assholes would even wear it to parties. Jesus, how stupid! Right?

Yes, it was only those who lived in Breña, Lince, La Victoria.

Karushansky's friends? No, we never got to know any of them but we sure would have liked to. Especially the gals...

He was always talking about Jewish broads, how sweet, how yummy they were. And us, is it true they put out? We weren't trying to be nasty, we had heard that Jewish girls weren't as square as Peruvian girls; they put out.

No, we didn't know any of them close up, personally, but we used to see them in the neighborhood once in a while—always kind of lost in their own locked-up, secret world. What are they like? we wondered then.

Karushansky himself was to blame, telling us all that crap. In summer, he told us, boys and girls pitched camp near Chosica. Two or three weeks all alone, without parents to check up on them. And did we know what it meant? Well, they all fucked like crazy! Seriously, it's what he used to tell us.

At night, according to him, they stood guard in pairs, a guy and a gal. And while the camp snored away... Well, we could imagine the rest. At this point the Jew would give us a knowing wink...

And each chick was sweeter and easier than the next one. Naturally it opened our appetites, we were dying to meet them. Could anyone go to the summer camp? we asked him one day. No, Karushansky said, you've got to be Jewish. Then, Brother, when are you going to throw a party at your house and introduce us? He said nothing, shied away from the answer. And then, just kidding, we insisted, D'you have any sisters? No? What a shame! Cousins? Yeah? How many? Are they nice? Why don't you introduce them to us? Okay, when is the party? If he asked his cousins we would take ours along, fair exchange, right? And at this point the Jew blew his top: Who did we think we were? His cousins weren't on the make. And us, C'mon, take it easy, brother, it was only a joke; we tried to play it down. But he shouldn't be so selfish either, no? After all, we always asked him to our parties.

Once, he said he'd invite us to his confirmation. First we had to meet at the synagogue for the ceremony, he said, and afterward we'd all go dancing at the Bolívar. It's going to be packed with genuine Jewish broads, he said, we could have our pick. But when the time came nothing happened. Weeks went by and the Jew not letting on till, one day, he popped up with the story that they'd already thrown the party for him. And how come you didn't let us know? What a fuck-up! And him, I couldn't, they had given the party during vacation, he was real sorry but he didn't even know where any of us lived, but there would be another time... It was always another time.

Why didn't he invite us? Who knows! Look, maybe it was his old man's fault, maybe he didn't want to ask us because we weren't Jews. Yeah, maybe that was it. You never can tell, right?

About him being thrown out of school: That was toward the end of the year. No, we don't exactly know what happened. Well, there was this rumor, they caught him and Aranzani in the barracks, fucking away...

Apparently Iron Ass caught them at it, after lunch, while we were all in the classrooms. He must have suspected something because he carried them off to the infirmary to examine them. That Jew had balls! Look, he stayed in the barracks with Montenegro on duty, isn't that something?

Yeah, nothing ever got past his nose. A bastard. On the day Iron Ass was on duty you had to go by the book: boots spit-and-polished, not a single button could be missing on our capes, knots in neckties had to be perfect. He would blow his whistle and all of us would start scrambling like mad. Exactly one minute for the year to fall in: and make sure not to wriggle around in ranks like sexed-up whores. Anybody who moved, wham! he was put on report right there—restricted on Saturday and Sunday and go take it up with the pope. Yeah, that's what he used to say.

We don't really know if he was expelled. When Karushansky came back that day from the infirmary, he said nothing; neither did Aranzani. But they disappeared about a week later without even taking their things. One afternoon, weeks later, when the whole year was in rank formation on the parade grounds, they made the announcement. They just said Karushansky and Aranzani had left school.

No, we never saw the Jew again. It was like the earth had swallowed him, no?

Yeah, he disappeared from the map...

FIVE

: Yes folks : Let's play ball! :

Long clearance by Gilmar to the midfield area : With Benítez marking him, Berkowitz traps the ball with the sole of his foot : He sends a back pass to Vavá : Over to Pelé : Señor Karushansky in center field, breaking away from his markers : in the center of *Lima my old Lima* : religiously on his way to the store, like every other day : every day from sunrise to sundown he's there behind the counter : measuring : cutting : selling cloth : because that is his only world : the store! : Not the nomadic Arab's bazaar he had years ago : portable, put together with stakes covered with skins to ward off the sun : No : Don Yehuda's world is a store standing on its own foundation : in the Mercado Central : right in the heart of a Lima that still clings to proud vestiges of viceregal days : And on his daily pilgrimage Don Yehuda feels himself being transported to the Holy Land : To Acre : where he is swallowed up in its market's maze of streets : arches and grilles : merchants sitting in the doorways of their stores : snake charmers : Arabs squatting like Peruvian Indians, their eyes lost in the waters of time : Yes, folks : the Lima of the old days : where despite his constant vowing to end his days in a kibbutz, Don Yehuda will be buried : DRINK INKA KOLA AND VISIT THE MUSEUM OF THE INQUISITION, FREE, ALL DAY EVERY DAY :

Brazil still has the ball : Pelé boots it high toward Peru's goal and Delgado heads it clear : Didí recovers for Brazil : Zito makes one of his typical blind-side runs up the far right : Didí passes him a through ball : it's marked danger! : Joe Calderón tries to cut it off but Zito gets it : Vavá running well to support, gets the ball from Zito and turns it over to Pelé : who fires a terrific cannon shot at the Peruvian goal : But Blackie Zegarra is positioned just right and hugs the ball to him like a spider! : Clapping and cheers from all sides of the stadium where there isn't even room for a pin to wedge itself in : What a festive air in José Díaz Stadium where every last Peruvian fan has met to celebrate the popular feast of Pesach! : In Egypt were we in bondage, the rabbi says, smiling as he sits down :

Zegarra throws a long pass to Joya over near the right sideline : He gives it to Terry : who kicks it to Marquitos in the half-moon zone just outside the penalty area : Tight man-to-man defense by the Brazilian team : Iron Ass marks Seminario : Berkowitz is on Vides Mosquera : Dr. Márquez on Terry :

and the rabbi on Marquitos : who dribbles past him neatly and tries to surprise the goalie with a powerful blast : But his mother makes an easy stop : However, we're sure things can't go on this way : All roads lead back home and so Marquitos will fire the ball at his mother again : We know Marquitos will go on a long voyage through history to return to his hometown : And here he is, almost home, waylaid by Father Camacho : who fouls him :

Didí takes the foul : He serves it to Rabbi Goldstein : But he loses the ball to Marquitos : who enters the eighteen-yard line of his hometown : His mother comes out trying to get to the ball: Marquitos chips the ball over her head and goal : Goooooal for Peru! : Sensational goal by Marquitos who caught the Brazilian goalie flatfooted! : His mother opened up the hole and Marquitos had no problem dipping the ball inside the left corner of the net : The stands are literally shaking with excitement! : Flags waving on all sides : Yessiree : You've got to know how to shoot : because as the Colonel, director of the military academy says, there's always the possibility of a war with Chile : Ecuador : or Colombia, it's all the same! : The score, 3 to 3 : But Peru cannot stand pat with a tie or let them take away Arica : Peru has to go all out for a victory now : To recover Palestine for the honor and glory of our people! : There's still plenty of time : We're only at the twenty-five-minute mark in the second half :

Brazil in possession of the ball : Pelé advances up the left side : He passes to old Karushansky : Fleming clears the ball well to the midfield area : Benítez picks it up : He sends a forward pass to

Seminario : Who feeds the ball back to him : This time Benítez gives it to Vides Mosquera : A high lob toward Marquitos : Marquitos gets a good fast start on the ball, with Rabbi Goldstein after him : Goldstein chops him down from behind and Marquitos falls over and goes rolling down the field of history : A confusing intertwined history the boy loses himself in : Abraham leaves the city of Ur with Manco Cápac and his wife Mama Ocllo close on his trail . . . : Rugged country : desolate plateaus, deserts : Adonai appears and says in a thundering voice : "Unto thy seed will I give this land" : And so the Sun, father of the Incas, seeing that men lived like beasts, takes pity and sends Manco Cápac to save them : He comes with his wife to Huanacaure Mountain, near Cuzco, and drives a golden wedge into the ground and founds the Empire : "Look now toward heaven and tell the stars, if thou be able to number them : So shall thy seed be" : Manco Cápac takes possession of the lands of the Sahuasiray and the Alcahuisas and Adonai appears and says to him : "This is my covenant : Every manchild among you shall be circumcised : And ye shall circumcise the flesh of your foreskin : and it shall be a token of the covenant betwixt me and you : And he that is eight days old shall be circumcised among you, every manchild in your generations, he that is born in the house, or bought with money of any stranger, which is not of thy seed" : Peru in possession and there's chaos on the playing field : Marquitos is all tangled up with the ball : Let's see now, list the fourteen Incas! : At one time, ladies and gentlemen, he could reel them off but now he stumbles on the seventh one : Who is he? : Pachacutec? : Tupak Yupanki? : And yet he has no trouble with the Jewish Prophets and Kings : He's got them all down pat : The same goes for the Twelve Tribes, from Reuben to Benjamin : Good Lord, he ought to be ashamed of himself! :

Lieutenant Montenegro does not call the foul and lets the ball continue in play : Sprawled on the grass, Marquitos is trying to get to his feet : he staggers a couple of steps toward the ball : then collapses on the turf again : A deathlike silence in the stadium! : Death is sneaking up on him : But have no fear : You will not die in your native land : another death lies in store for you : There is a difference between dying like Trumpeldor and dying like Leoncio Prado, isn't there? Our cameras are now rushing to Huánuco to cover the death of the Peruvian hero and patron of our school : He asks for a cup of coffee before being executed : then he gives the signal : two little taps on the cup : and pow, pow, Leoncio Prado is dead : a martyr at the hands of the Chileans : DRINK SOL DE ICA : THE PISCO THAT CHEERS YOUR SPIRIT AND GIVES YOUR HEART A LIFT :

There is Marquitos, the victim of a treacherous injury, writhing in pain in the school infirmary : The doctor on duty pulls on his gloves : Montenegro orders him to assume the right-angle position : To drop his pants and bend over : The stadium's loudspeakers announce that Tito Drago is coming in to take the boy's place : What a lousy break for Peru : The referee tells the players to get on with the game, while someone announces from downstairs that Marquitos is receiving emergency treatment in the infirmary : With him, Cadet Aranzani, a real cutie with his Sandra Dee babyface : Lieutenant Montenegro, lanky, sporting a Clark Gable mustache, informs the doctor :

"These cadets have been screwing in the Fifth Year barracks" :

They order Marquitos to take his clothes off and sit on the chamber pot : But this won't do, fans, because everybody knows Marquitos can't strip in front of his friends! : Peruvian or Jewish : So he hides behind some shrubbery : A pecker in hand is worth two in the bush! : And every Jew worth his salt must go to the camp : Every Jew must get close to the soil : Going, if not to the kibbutz, at least to the Betar camp : The referee orders him to change his clothes and Marquitos hides behind the tent : He will not let anyone see his pecker, no way : Life has played a mean trick on him and he can't do what he has always wanted to do : whip it out in front of his friends to show he's Jewish too : as Jewish as they are : Because if he does, they'll laugh their heads off : "It looks like a little strip of cow leather," Dr. Berkowitz smirks : he is talking about the red star-shaped blotch that covers the glans : Yes folks : the Mongolian spot! : the test of the true-blue Peruvian! : AND DRINK INKA KOLA : THE NATIONAL BRAND REFRESHMENT :

Standing with his arms crossed, Iron Ass never takes his eyes off him : Marquitos clenches his fists hard, straining and pushing : A painful scene for the Peruvian squad, playing without Marquitos :

"Finish your bowel movement so they can examine your asshole," Montenegro says :

Vides has the ball : He delivers to Tito Drago :

Tito crosses the eighteen-yard line : He has a chance to shoot : And it's hard to see how but he boots the ball wide and the referee indicates goal kick for Brazil : The ball goes to Pelé : 3 to 3 on the scoreboard : The sphere is in Peruvian territory : Señor Karushansky goes up into the air: he heads the ball : and Zegarra barely manages to deflect it, producing a corner : Rabbi Goldstein switches the ball to his other foot and lobs a low cross : Delgado tries to kick it clear but misses and the ball rolls around loose in the penalty zone : There's a mixup in Peru's defense : Soria finally makes a last-minute clearance and the linesman signals throw-in for Brazil : The Peruvian team is a shambles again! : Playing by fits and starts : There's a worried expression on Coach Muñoz's face, he can't figure out why, with what right, Professor Refugio Cuevas orders them to take Marquitos to the Psychopedagogic Department at León Pinelo :

> "The trouble is," Commentator Cuevas says, "Marquitos is trying to corrupt our school : He molests the girls : plays with their asses : their tits : And we certainly cannot stand for that" :

Is that why Don Yehuda pulls him out of the game and puts him into the Leoncio Prado Academy? : That's the point in question at this moment when Peru has to go all out to win the game : Don Yehuda is now entering the dressing room and quickly fires at Marquitos :

> "Now we going live in rooming house near the store : You go in boarding school : I put you in Leoncio Prado : Is good school : you going have everything there you need" :

This shot blasts Marquitos in the chest and goes out of bounds : Throw-in for Brazil : Didí receives and breaks away fast from the man covering him : A short push-pass to Vavá : Garrincha makes a check-off run up the right side : Peru's defense closes ranks, North and South : Facing the goal, Señor Karushansky heads the ball and it hits the left post and bounces back onto the field : The Peruvian team looks terrible without Marquitos! : If we could only go back to the good old days with our buddies in La Victoria : hometown of the Alianza Lima team! : The notorious Black Steamroller : to the days of black stars like Magallanes, Manguera Villanueva, and José María Lavalle : The Three Wise Men of the Covenant : Gunn, Rapaport, and Rajman! : who, now that the sun is beginning to go down behind our stadium, come to Marquitos's hometown bearing gifts : Between them, they carry the glittering Star of David! : Gunn places the chain around the boy's neck with great ceremony :

"You are now one of us," he announces in a voice loaded with meaning :

"Never take it off," Samuelito adds :

But listen folks, by the next day chain and star have ended up at the bottom of the river and that night Marquitos dreams that three gypsies with glowing eyes come to the foot of his bed to demand an explanation : Here in our booth to tell us all about Marquitos's injury is doctor, Belisario Márquez :

> "It would be premature to try to give a diagnosis of the injury before we carry out a more thorough examination :
>
> However, we can say now that it is serious : His

muscles show signs of dilation and there's a slight irregularity in the connective tissue : We can give a similar diagnosis of Cadet Aranzani's condition, but in his case the dilation in the rectum is much more evident : much wider" :

Fans, we can breathe easy again : We haven't the slightest doubt that Marquitos will come back into this crucial game any minute now : In effect, Lieutenant Montenegro stops the action and orders Marquitos to come onto the field : Tito Drago leaves and Marquitos Karushansky Ávila comes in! : Peruvian flags waving to and fro on all sides : Brazil is ready to take its free kick : The serve goes to the rabbi : He puts too much on the ball, and it's a throw-in for Peru : Joya breaks away fast up the right side : Terry and Marquitos in midfield : Vides Mosquera also moves into position : Ball to Marquitos who slips : Very closely marked by the defensive trio Berkowitz-Goldstein-Karushansky : He shields the ball well with his body : Gets to his feet : Has no trouble shaking off his three rivals and sets the ball up for a shot : he kicks and the ball shaves the post and goes out : A ball, ladies and gentlemen, carrying bad news for Marquitos's mother! Her son is dying STOP : Critical infection produced by Neisser's gonococcus STOP : Will circumcise him STOP : Will perform Bar Mitzvah STOP : He's about to be expelled from Leoncio Prado Academy STOP : And be packed off to Israel STOP :

The referee halts all action and awards a free kick to Peru : Marquitos gets the pass in the clear : he connects with his left and leaves the fans in the stands with the word *Gooooooal* stuck in their throats : This deadlock has to break any minute now! : Go, go, go, boys, on to victory! : Pass the ball to Marquitos : Let him take the ball into the Brazilian goal fiercely defended by his mother : But Marquitos fouls Pelé! : Lieutenant Montenegro calls it : The school's Colonel comes over to take the kick : He rips all the insignia from Marquitos's uniform : They'll blow the whistle on him and kick him out of the game : His father will die of shame : Señor Yehuda Karushansky : born in Bessarabia : came with his suitcase on his shoulder to Peru, land of beautiful sierras, snow-capped peaks, and breath-taking waterfalls, *oh my Peru*! :

And yet they can't possibly throw Marquitos out of the game before the final whistle : Not even if his ship is ready to weigh anchor and his father is getting his handkerchief ready : First, Marquitos will save us from defeat : He will save our country's honor as only he can, as he did against Uruguay, dropping two precious goals between Manon's snow-white thighs : And there he is now, going through a hole in the Brazilian defense, to creep into Manon's room : his little cousin Raquel's? : or Cadet Aranzani's? : No folks : it's a reverse action play : It's Shoshana, Hebrew virgin princess, coming into Marquitos's room, in the small hours of the night : Silence in the stands : Shadows begin to flood the stadium : And here is Shoshana, begging, pleading with him, in a voice breaking with modesty, not to be so mean : to let her see his circumcised member with its Mongolian star : Marquitos tells the girl to get out of the playing field : Tries to push her out : But Shoshana gets a stranglehold on his arm : they tussle : Marcos can't get away : he surrenders : Shoshana still won't let go : Her cheeks are on fire : There's a gentle smile on her lips : and a warm intense radiance in her eyes : All of a sudden he feels something pulling him toward her and their bodies rub : a tingling sensation starts in the pit of his stomach : She brings her lips close and Marcos feels a warm breath on his face and against his chest the girl's tiny pointed nipples hardening under her blouse : He relaxes and she kisses him again, parting her lips, rolling her warm, frothy tongue : And their mouths suddenly meet : he feels himself being sucked under and lets himself go spinning deep into a bottomless hole : He is on top of her now, running his hands over her body, pulling her skirt down, and there's her bare midriff : her pants next, and there's her curly bush : and his nervous hands going around the girl's waist, feeling her thighs : and their mouths mingle in one breath : they're panting and struggling for air : How well Marquitos carries the ball! : Watch him making his move, head high, dropping his trousers, his shirt : Their two bodies lock : Tangled in dangerous play : his erect member, insistent, trying to drill through Shoshana's defense : her moist, spongy pubis : Marquitos goes on driving through midfield : He sinks into the girl's body : a warm, sticky liquid flows out weakly : A frantic struggle in the final eighteen yards : Their bodies are still coupled, oscillating on one axle : He pumps and squeezes her very hard, trapped between desire and a kind of rage, as if an urgent furious need to get even were spurring him on : to get even? : for what? : with whom? : He doesn't know : Shreds of memories float in his head, crisscrossing, stopping him from hitting on the exact object of his fury : Naturally the referee calls a foul against Marquitos's mother who bravely rushes out to meet her son's violent charge :

Yes folks : nothing can compare to the Jewish woman! : And here to prove it, making her grand entrance into our stadium, is glamorous Gladys Zender, just recently crowned Miss Universe in Palm Beach : the first and only miss to wear this crown in our country's long history, for the greater honor of Peru and the ancient people of Israel : And now the new St. Rose of Lima by the grace of Adonai, Gladys enters in a carriage of the colonial era, worthy of a queen, to go once around inside the stadium, met by wild applause and a steady shower of carnations and gardenias from the stands : Long live Peru! : Long live the people of Israel! :

The ball is in play : Come on Peru! : Marquitos carries the ball : Dr. Berkowitz stands in his way holding a needle in front of him : Marquitos backpedals, lobbing the ball to Fleming who is far up the field : Ball over to the left side : The Lima sun is starting to sink out of sight : We need more light in this stadium now that night is throwing its black crepe mantle over the grounds and we're moving into the last minutes of the game : Vides is dribbling the ball in Brazilian territory : Let there be light!, the stadium's loudspeakers announce : And there is light! : The ball goes back to Seminario : Someone grabs him from behind : foul : The referee awards Peru a free kick : DON'T SAY BEER : SAY CRISTAL : THE CHAMPION OF BEERS :

Long deep ball over to Marquitos : He's coming to the Holy Land : Haifa's lights come into view like the glittering letters of a golden alphabet : The entire Peruvian team has launched a last-ditch attack deep into enemy territory : Forty-two minutes of play in the second half : Now the referee calls a foul committed by Marquitos against his father : This is outrageous! : Lieutenant Montenegro gives Marquitos a warning : Scared out of his wits, Peru's inside wing tries to break away up the left side : We have to score again! : To pull this game out of the fire, come hell or high water! : So, lieutenant sir, don't ask him to bend over : Doctor, don't examine his asshole : At least wait for time to be up and for Peru to clinch a victory : No, sir : those are orders from Lieutenant Montenegro : Marquitos recovers the ball : Exactly one minute for the game to end : The lieutenant is about to turn his report in to the Colonel : Marquitos advances with the leather : His mother is well situated in the goalmouth : His father raises his handkerchief : Marquitos is now inside the eighteen-yard line of foreign territory : He gets ready to shoot : when, ladies and gentlemen, Lieutenant Montenegro looks at his watch and blows the whistle and the game is over . . . :

EPILOGUE
that may also serve as prologue

President Chaim Weizmann died in Israel that week.

And at once, the entire Jewish community in Lima went into mourning, with memorial ceremonies held everywhere. The first one was at the León Pinelo, then still at its old site on Húsares de Junín. The following evening the memorial went on to the synagogue on Iquique, where Betar, one of two Zionist youth clubs (the other was Hanoar), also stood. Most members, especially the younger ones, were unaware of Betar's ideological ties with Herut, the Israeli party whose slogan called for a Jewish nation on both sides of the Jordan.

All this took place in the early fifties, before the synagogue on Brazil Avenue was built and the León Pinelo moved to its new site on Orrantia del Mar.

The old building would be turned over to Hanoar and the synagogue on Iquique would go to Betar, all but one section of the upper floor, which became a sanctuary for the evening prayers of ten or twelve cats that usually congregated there.

That same week of Weizmann's death, Marquitos Karushansky arrived in Lima. Behind him he was leaving a childhood of lean but happy days. In the home of his grandparents, where eleven children were squeezed into two small bedrooms and where no one found it strange that the living room had never been furnished or used by any of its members, the family lived under the black cloud of poverty, thanks to the grandfather's avarice. Totally absorbed in his activities of street peddler and moneylender—and making of stinginess a virtue—the old man's contact with his house was that of a shadow passing through. His real life, from sunrise to sundown, except for return forays for replenishment, was in the streets where he could be seen with a bundle of merchandise under one arm, tramping from door to door or selling his wares on any street corner. But he showed up religiously each evening to preside over the dinner table. And no one could start eating until he took his place at the head of the table and gave the signal, his only display of authority over the family throughout his life. With it, his body appeared to take on a more solid form, but it lasted only through the meal, because the minute he left the table, he turned into a shadow once more.

In the house, his grandson alone saw him under a different light. Marquitos would never be able to forget the picture of the old man in the back room stacking his coins. From the dinner table, the grandfather would go straight into the room where he kept his strongbox and there he would spill the day's profits on a table and count his earnings by the light of a candle. He didn't seem to be much interested in the paper money: he jotted down its total in a crumbling little notebook, trussed the bills with a rubber band, and put them away safely in the strongbox. And from it he would take a leather pouch whose contents he would pour out on the table in small spurts, his eyes dancing with delight. When the stream of coins ran out, his nimble fingers would settle down to business: little stacks sprouted everywhere as if by magic. He counted them, knocked them down, and built them up again. During this performance—and this was the image engraved on his mind—Marquitos saw him go through a transformation and take on a presence that was even more solid than when he sat down at table with his air of authority.

By opening for him the doors of his secret world, his grandfather made him a silent partner in avarice as well as loneliness. Furthermore, since the boy was the son of a Jew, the old man may have believed that he had found an ally who could appreciate, even if only through instinct, his own passion for money. He did not have the same conviction about his wife and his children. He had not pinned his hopes on any of them, not even on the youngest ones, and with them all he remained at arm's length, as if by a tacit understanding: he and they lived together yet were completely invisible to each other most of the time. And it was only at his death (it coincided with Marcos's departure for Israel in 1962) that his sons were able to see him as a whole person for the first time. On the day of his burial—one could almost say it was their way of giving vent to the rage they had been holding back, for years—not one of them followed the old man's body to the cemetery. On that same day, an anonymous hand added a special finishing touch to his tomb with this caustic but well-earned epitaph: "In his eyes the world had the roundness of a coin."

Some weeks before his grandfather died, Marcos showed up in town. Ten years after leaving, he was returning not only to say goodbye to his mother but also with a strange mission his father had given him: to go to the home of the priest (he and old Karushansky had been close, at one time), ask him for a crate of avocados, and take it back with him to Lima: "Following the river you get there in ten maybe fifteen minutes. If you wait till sun sets, you can walk in shade of eucalyptus trees."

After almost twenty years of absence, his father still remembered that the best avocados in the area grew in the priest's orchard: "They are gems. No others like them in thirty maybe forty kilometers around. If he offers them free, take and thank him; otherwise pay him. Here's some money."

Marcos went to see him. Having retired a few years back, he lived with a sister, who had never married, outside of town on the road to the old ice and storage house. He had been his childhood parish priest but Marcos did not recognize him. With his crown of thick white hair, and wearing his old cassock, the priest, who was sprawled out in a rocking chair whose back looked like the bridge of a ship, seemed to be floating in the dim light of the room. He had lost most of his vision and his memory was almost as clouded as his eyes.

"What did you say your father's name was?"

It was the fourth or fifth time he had asked this question.

"Karushansky. Don Yehuda Karushansky."

"A tall, hulking, red-faced man who worked at the Las Cruces mill and lived on Arequipa Street?"

Marcos said no.

"Then it must be the man who had the barber shop. It was in the Plaza de Armas and got burned down."

"No. Not him either," the boy said.

"Ah, then it has to be the Hungarian who was found knifed at the bottom of the river! Of course, he left a string of children all over the place..."

But Marcos said no again. And before he could say anything else, the priest broke in: "Shhh! Don't tell me, I'm starting to remember."

And he sank deeper into the rocking chair: a frown on his face, as if he were straining hard to sort out his memories. And so as not to drive them off, he stayed in the same position a long time, stretched out, holding his breath. At last he raised his head and tried to rivet Marcos's eyes with his own dull whitish ones. The boy started. He turned his eyes away. The walls were reflecting the last strands of the evening sun. He felt sticky sweat crawling down his back like spider legs. And then he heard the priest's voice, coming from far away.

Like the river's rumble. As if he were saying a prayer. But he did not look at him. And with his eyes half closed, not stopping to look at anything, he felt his way out of the house. Only later, when he got back into town, did he remember the avocados. He had not mentioned them to Father Camacho, because of that famous orchard his father remembered as a second Garden of Eden, nothing remained, not even a shadow.